A S

After a broken romance, Dr Kate Murray found comfort in her work in a busy Yorkshire general practice. It was a pity, though, that there was no way she could avoid the insufferable surgeon Angus McGill, or stop his infuriating interference in her life!

Having written fiction and non-fiction for children of all ages for many years, Jennifer Eden turned to writing Doctor Nurse Romances first as a challenge, then with increasing enjoyment as a new creative world opened up for her. She is very lucky in having a good back-up team of a husband and two sons with medical and dental qualifications. Having also experienced the other side of medicine as a patient, she hopes she is able to convey something of that with understanding too. Jennifer Eden has written three other Doctor Nurse Romances, *Nurse on Approval*, *Stop-Gap Doctor* and *Surgeon in Retreat*.

A SURGEON'S HANDS

BY

JENNIFER EDEN

MILLS & BOON LIMITED
15-16 BROOK'S MEWS
LONDON W1A 1DR

First published in Great Britain 1986
by Mills & Boon Limited

© Jennifer Eden 1986

Australian copyright 1986
Philippine copyright 1986

ISBN 0 263 75635 1

Set in Linotron Times 10 on 11 pt.
03-0187-48963

Typeset in Great Britain by
Associated Publishing Services
Printed and bound in Great Britain by
Collins, Glasgow

CHAPTER ONE

BEFORE she had started on her first glass of champagne Kate was thinking, much against her will, how lovely the bride looked. After she finished it she decided that the bride looked more like a fairy off a Christmas tree. By the time she had downed her third glass, too quickly after the other two, she saw with extraordinary clarity that the bride was over-dressed, over made-up and over-queening all around her, including the groom, who looked increasingly uneasy. The newly created Mrs Martin Earle didn't intend to be eclipsed by anyone on *her* wedding day!

It was an impressive reception being held in the grounds of Hill House, the home of Mr and Mrs Barker, the bride's parents. They were now going the rounds of their guests, exuding bonhomie and well-heeled cordiality. No expense had been spared for their only daughter, and if Mrs Barker dropped an aitch occasionally and Mr Barker came out with an inopportune 'mate', nobody noticed. The Barkers were so extrovertly happy that their good humour infected their guests.

Only Kate watched their progress with a jaundiced eye and she had her reasons. From the depth of her heart she wished they had stayed in London where they had made their dubious wealth, but twelve months ago they had arrived in Yelverthorpe, one

of the loveliest old market towns in north-east
Yorkshire, and had bought Hill House, a mock-
Tudor mansion, and then proceeded to furnish it
with antiques, outbidding even the dealers at local
sales.

When they had finished buying property they
started on people, poaching gardeners and cooks
and daily women from their neighbours with offers
of higher wages.

All this could have made the Barkers very
unpopular, but they were so generous and good-
tempered that any resentment towards them soon
melted away. All except Kate's—but then they had
also acquired Martin for their daughter, in spite of
the fact that he was then engaged to Kate.

Sandra had fallen in love with him at first sight
and wanted him—that was sufficient reason. And
Martin and Kate, the Barkers argued, were only
childhood sweethearts—they hadn't given each other
a chance to meet anyone else—calf-love couldn't be
taken seriously. They weren't quite right in that
assumption; Kate and Martin had been teenagers,
not children, when they first met. The Barkers
squared their consciences by telling everybody they
were doing the young couple a favour, breaking up
a relationship that was only born of habit, but how
did Martin square *his* conscience? Kate asked
herself.

She watched him now through narrowed greeny-
grey eyes—her one claim to beauty; their shape and
colour were enough to turn heads—and her anger
and hurt pride was overcome by a hopeless longing.
How many times had she seen him like that, an
expression of patient boredom marring his handsome
features—in lecture halls, the common room, even
the examination hall. His boredom threshold was

very low. She knew his faults and loved him in spite of them, had loved him since she had first met him, eight years before when she, like him, had been a new student at the medical school.

His looks alone had singled him out from fellow students—tall, slight, extremely dark, with liquid brown eyes under a long sweep of dark lashes that were the envy of most girls.

'Have you seen the new Adonis?' Carole Bircham, another first-year student, had asked. 'Those eyes—that classical nose. Pity about the weak chin, though.'

'I think it's a shapely chin,' Kate had retorted. She couldn't fault him in any way.

'He could always grow a beard, I suppose—but not to worry about the chin—just look at those eyes!' said Carole flippantly. 'If he were a sheikh and ogled me over his yashmak, I'd go into his tent any time!'

'Isn't it the sheikh's wife who wears the yashmak?' said Kate, feigning ignorance, and giggling, the two girls walked away together. Kate didn't expect to see much of the handsome young medic in the future—the competition would be too keen.

But circumstances were to prove otherwise, for Kate and Martin naturally drifted into each other's company, they were the two best brains of their year. Most of the honours and prizes were shared between them and what started as a friendly rivalry ended up a committed love.

Martin wanted to get married, but that was impractical as they both relied on grants and holiday jobs to cover their expenses as students. The other alternative, living together, Kate wouldn't even consider. She told herself that that kind of involvement would hamper their chances of a career later. Supposing there was a child, for instance? Then too, there was Simon to think of.

Simon was her brother, seven years her junior and very dependent upon her as she had had sole care of him since their mother died when he was fourteen. Memories of her father were vague, for he had left home when Simon was little more than a year old and her mother had never mentioned his name again and had destroyed all photographs of him.

Kate dragged herself away from the past, and once more looked across at Martin. This time their eyes met. A look flared in his face that reminded her of the old days, when they had been younger, full of hopes and plans, and desperately poor. A smart jacket in the window of a men's outfitters, a sports car roaring past, sometimes even just a smile from her, could bring that look into his eyes. She called it his yearning look and teased him about it. It came when he saw something he couldn't have, and it was there now and he was looking at her!

Kate turned her head, knowing the dip in her hat brim would hide her face. If Martin still loved her why had he married Sandra? Not for the money—she couldn't bring herself to believe that. Years ago she had conceded that Carole had been right about his chin, it did denote weakness, but when you love someone you love them faults and all, and he had other virtues that made up for a few failings.

He was hard-working and ambitious. When Kate went into general practice to make the extra money needed to help Simon in turn through medical school, Martin had stayed on at the hospital to study for a specialist's degree. It didn't occur to her then that she was subsidising his keep. He had most of his meals at the small flat she and Simon shared;

he brought her his washing and mending to deal with and she loved making herself useful to him. She delighted in having two to mother instead of one.

Marriage was no longer mentioned. It was taken for granted that they would delay it until Simon was qualified, and if Kate guessed that the casual flirtations Martin indulged in were not so innocent as they appeared, she kept the knowledge hidden away with her other disappointments.

'Would you mind if I shared this table with you? It's away from where all the noise is and it's pleasant here under the trees.' A booming voice broke in on her thoughts, and she turned with a show of impatience to face a broad, heavily-built man with massive shoulders and a lot of coarse red hair. She took him for the gardener.

Kate tried, not very successfully, to hide her annoyance. She had chosen this table well away from the other guests so that she could watch Martin without being observed. And she did draw the line at having to sit with someone so disreputable-looking, especially when she had taken such care with her own appearance.

The newcomer, who had the deepest blue irises she had ever seen, twinkled unashamedly at her. He had shaggy, overhanging brows that accentuated his deep-set eyes, his nose and mouth were large. Everything about him was large, particularly his voice, and he looked tanned and weatherbeaten. A farmer perhaps, not the gardener—and obviously a guest, judging by the way he lolled in the chair at ease.

He surveyed the scene before them with a cynical eye. A large marquee had been erected to house the buffet table and the bar. Waitresses in candy-striped dresses and starched aprons flitted backwards and forwards from guests to marquee like little pink bees to their hive. A waiter was in charge of the drinks and two stewards went the rounds with trays. The tables that dotted the lawn around the marquee had pink cloths over them and there were covers the same colour on the chairs.

Though the sun was still high in the heavens the fairy lights threaded among the trees were lit up, so was the concealed lighting in the ornate fountain. A narrow strip of red carpet led from the marquee across the lawn, up the steps of the terrace and into the house. Along this the wedding party were now proceeding like royalty at a reception.

'Well, well!' came the hearty voice of the interloper again. 'I see there's nothing lacking that money and bad taste can't supply.' He grinned at Kate, showing strong white teeth. 'No offence intended. You're not a relative, I trust?'

'Just a friend,' she retorted stiffly.

'A friend of the groom?' And in answer to her questioning look, 'I just guessed, by the way you looked at him, as if you had a proprietorial right.'

'We were at college together.'

'I see.' And he did too, she realised that by the way his large mouth curved into a knowing smile. Were her feelings so patently obvious that this coarse stranger could guess them at a glance? Her hands had been gripping the table's edge, now she quickly hid them in her lap. The white band of flesh where Martin's ring had been showed up against the rest of her finger. Anybody could read the signs—anybody could put two and two together.

When she had first received the gold-embossed invitation to the wedding Kate had thought it a sick joke. Nobody with an ounce of sensitivity could inflict *that* upon her. Then Martin had phoned, begging her to accept. 'I'll need you,' he had said. 'Just knowing you're there will help me through the day. Please, Kate, you've never let me down before.'

She had replaced the receiver, hardly able to believe her ears. Martin needed *her* on the day he was marrying his blonde-haired, blue-eyed fairy doll! What did he think she was made of! More to the point—what kind of man was he to make such a request of her?

Later, thinking about it quietly, she looked back over the years and realised she had always been there when Martin wanted her, sometimes at great inconvenience to herself. Times when he was troubled or worried, or sometimes just wanting her there in the lecture theatre when he was assisting at an operation. She always had to be in the background giving him the moral support he expected.

Perhaps that was where she had gone wrong. If she had been less of a sister to Martin, more of a lover, would he have left her for Sandra? It was too late to ask herself that now.

One of the wine stewards approached and she took her fourth glass of champagne from the proffered tray. The man opposite raised a quizzical eyebrow.

'I think I'd better get you something to eat to help that down. We seem to be missed out here, too far away. What do they call you, girlie?'

'Katrina Anne Murray,' replied Kate with a slightly slurred dignity.

'What a mouthful! I bet you're known as Kate.'

'Only by my friends!'

'Right, Kate, I won't be long,' and off he ambled, moving decepti ely fast with a rolling unhurried-looking gait.

Kate glared after him, wondering if her legs would support her if she got up and walked away, but didn't feel sure enough to try. An attractive young woman in her early thirties came up to the table.

'Who's that self-opinionated gorilla?' Kate asked truculently, nodding towards the figure heading in the direction of the refreshment marquee.

Rachel Wiles pushed the glass of champagne out of Kate's reach before seating herself on the vacant chair. She was slight and dark and had known Kate for the past two years, ever since Kate had joined the Yelverthorpe practice, in fact. Rachel was a vet, in partnership with her father, and besides healing the sick had other things in common with Kate. She knew all about Martin, she knew too that under her glacier-like exterior Kate was a cauldron of boiling emotions.

'You're looking very smart,' she said. She admired Kate for looking her best, going down with flags flying as it were. Kate had on a cream silk dress, very plain and very stylish, and round her neck a long rope of black beads. Her straw hat, as fine as lace, was also black—as were her shoes, bag and gloves. Her smart simplicity made the other guests look like full-blown roses, in Rachel's opinion.

'I shaid—who's that gorilla!' Kate repeated, then hiccuped.

'That, my dear, is Angus McGill, and I shouldn't let him hear you refer to him as a gorilla if I were you. Don't be deceived by his lazy manner, he can be very fearsome when he likes.'

'And who is Angus McGill to come to a wedding dreshed as a tramp!'

'Himself. He does his own thing, as they say, but he can be a very snappy dresser when likes. He's an oral surgeon by profession, much respected locally, and he also has a medical degree, so don't be put off by his appearance. He's just returned from a two-year stint in Nigeria helping to organise an oral surgical unit in one of the new hospitals. Now he's back as head of the dental department at the District Hospital.' Rachel dropped her hectoring tone and looked keenly at her friend. 'How are you coping, Kate?'

'I'm not. I want to scream at the top of my voice, or hit out at someone or just sit here and howl. It hurts, Rachel—oh, my God it hurts!—but you've been through it too, you understand.'

Fleetingly a shadow crossed Rachel's thin, dark face. Her husband had walked out on her when Benjamin was three years old. That was five years ago and she still felt his loss. She stretched across the table and squeezed Kate's arm.

'If it's any consolation the hurt eases up after a time.' She would liked to have added—'And we're both well rid of a couple of bastards,' only that wouldn't have helped either Kate or herself.

Kate's beautiful almond-shaped eyes filled with alcoholic tears. 'And to think I brought it on myself inviting Martin up here for Christmas! If only I'd gone down to London instead. If only we hadn't gone to that Christmas Eve dance at the Town Hall—if only we hadn't met the Barkers. Sandra had her talons in him from that moment. Oh, if only—if only—if only—!' she slumped in her chair.

'Darling, what you need is to go home and sleep this off,' said Rachel, picking up the half-empty glass of champagne. 'I'll take this with me, it's heady stuff especially on an empty stomach, and I don't suppose you've had any lunch. Well, here comes your cavalier back again, and he looks as if he's brought you something to eat.'

Rachel went off before Angus McGill arrived. He came up, holding two well-filled plates in one hand and a pint tankard of beer in the other.

'I'm glad Des Barker had the sense to get in a keg of Yorkshire bitter,' he remarked, sliding one of the plates across to Kate. 'More suitable for a man than a glass of fancy bubbles. Here, get yourself round that, it'll bring some colour back to your face.'

Kate looked at the food with distaste. It was a mixture of caviar, smoked salmon, pate, cold meats and salad. 'I can't eat that!'

'Why not? I picked out the best.'

'I'm a vegetarian,' she told him. 'I never eat meat or fish.'

He stared at her open-mouthed. 'So you're a crank too! Well, well, it takes all sorts, I suppose, but I'm not going to waste good food, I'll eat it. I've been forking over in the garden all morning, and worked up quite an appetite.'

Kate watched him eat with an increasing aversion. Every movement he made grated on her nerves. He was a rapid eater—there was a saying—'fast eaters, fast workers'; this man could have set a record. Yet, and it was a reluctant yet, she noticed that his hands, in contrast to the rest of his appearance, were well looked after and the nails beautifully manicured. If she had looked at those first she would never have mistaken him for a manual worker. They were a surgeon's hands, broad and powerful with long strong fingers.

The waitresses brought round coffee. Kate liked hers strong and black, this was weak and milky, but she was glad of it. The effects of the champagne were wearing off and her inner despair was beginning to show in her expression and her bearing. Her hands trembled a little as she replaced her cup on its saucer, and she surprised a look of pity in the deep blue eyes watching her. She bristled.

'I think I'll go and see the honeymooners off,' she said, rising a little unsteadily to her feet. It was one way of escaping that vigilant regard.

Martin had changed from his formal grey morning dress into a light-coloured gaberdine suit. Sandra was still wearing unrelieved white, except for the single pink rose pinned to her bodice. A heavy gold bracelet which was a present from her father was round one wrist, and a slender gold chain which Martin had given her round her throat. Her fine floss-like hair sparkled in the sun, but her china-blue eyes were cold and uninterested. Something had obviously put her in a bad humour. She saw Kate among the other well-wishers, but walked past, ignoring her, leaving Kate to wonder if she was the unwitting cause of her annoyance.

Martin came up to her. His mouth was twitching at the corners, which she knew was a sign of nervous tension, but then that was a common complaint with bridegrooms, she couldn't read more into it than that.

'Thank you for coming, Kate,' he said in an undertone. 'I hope you'll wish me luck.'

'You'll need it,' she couldn't resist saying, and he answered dully,

'I know, that's why your good wishes mean so much to me.'

She hated herself for being so weak, for feeling

so sorry for him, for wanting to comfort him even now. She saw the same ache in his eyes and couldn't bear it.

'Please go, Martin, go now,' she said brokenly, 'before I make an utter fool of myself.'

A hired white Rolls-Royce was waiting in the drive to take the bridal pair to the airport. They were going to Alicante for their honeymoon, a place Martin would once have avoided at all costs, but Sandra loved the sun, glorying in the patina of pale gold it gave to her fair skin. They were driven away amid shrieks of goods wishes and some doubtful advice from Mr Barker's more bucolic friends, leaving the drive strewn with confetti and rose petals. Kate walked trance-like back to the table where she had left her bag.

She saw with misgiving that Angus McGill was still sitting there; she had hoped that in the interim he might have gone. He was slumped forward over his unfinished meal and at first sight she thought he was asleep.

As she drew nearer she noticed that he was shivering violently, and perspiration had broken out on his face like drops of dew. She realised he was in the throes of a severe rigor, and remembered Rachel saying he had spent two years in Nigeria. He might have contracted malaria there—perhaps suffered from recurring bouts. Kate hurried forward to feel his pulse.

It was as rapid as his breathing, all the same he mustered up enough strength to give her a wolfish grin, and said through chattering teeth, 'Playing at nurses, Kate?'

'Save your breath, I'm a doctor. Have you got any quinine tablets with you, or chloroquine?'

'Didn't think I'd need them, Doc, I had one of

these attacks only a fortnight ago—didn't expect
another so soon. Can you help me to my car?'

'Don't be so ridiculous, you're not fit to drive. I'll
help you to mine.'

'The perfect bedside manner,' he muttered feebly.
With a superhuman effort he got to his feet. Kate
marvelled at his will-power; most men would have
collapsed by now.

'I'd better get help—you can't walk,' she said
anxiously.

'I'm the best judge of that, I'm also a doctor,' his
breathing was so rapid it pushed his words out in
spurts. 'Give me your shoulder to lean on, I'll make
it to the car. I know a short cut to the road.'

The cars belonging to guests were parked in a
side lane. It was an agonising journey for them
both, and there was no question of saying goodbye
to their hosts first. Though he wasn't much taller
than she Angus McGill was extremely heavy, all
bone and muscle, and he stumbled along with his
full weight resting on her. She knew if he fell she
would never get him to his feet again.

By the time they reached the car they were both
soaked through, Angus from ague and Kate with
perspiration. His breathing was heavy and stertorous,
and alarming. Kate hadn't studied tropical medicine
in depth and had only an elementary knowledge of
malaria, but she did know there were several
different types and hoped fervently that this wasn't
the deadly *Plasmodium falciparum* variety. She
didn't care much for Angus McGill, but neither did
she wish him harm.

It took her several minutes to get him into the
passenger seat of her small car, and by this time he
was almost unconscious and a dead weight. How
she got him in finally, and even fastened the safety

belt around him, she didn't know. She too seemed
to be imbued with a superhuman strength; the
human body had strange stocks of reserve when the
need arose. But her legs were beginning to feel like
jelly when, breathless, she slid in behind the steering
wheel.

She felt too weak to drive off immediately. She
rested with her head on the steering wheel, taking
great gulps of air, making nearly as much noise
with her breathing as the man beside her. Presently
he stirred, and when she looked at him she saw that
his eyes were open and trying to focus.

'Did I pass out?' he muttered.

'Just for a few minutes.'

'It's this damn headache—I feel as if I have a
sledgehammer beating away inside my skull. Would
you have an aspirin on you?'

'You need quinine, not aspirin,' she told him.
'Where do you live, I'll get you home as quickly as
possible.'

'I live in Damgate just off the square in
Yelverthorpe, and I *do* need an aspirin, blast your
eyes!'

'I can tell you're feeling better,' Kate said dryly,
but she took two aspirins from a container in her
handbag and gave them to him. There was no water
to help them down, so he crunched the tablets
between his teeth.

He was far from recovery, she could tell that as
she drove carefully along the lanes to the town. His
breathing was still rapid and his head lolled forward
on his chest as if he were too weak to support it.
She could feel the heat of the fever that was burning
him up, and once, changing gear, her arm brushed
his and she recoiled at the touch. He seemed on
fire.

They reached Yelverthorpe through an estate of new houses, then narrow streets of small shops, finally the lopsided cobbled square. Kate knew Damgate, she sometimes took Pesky down there for a walk. It was a street of graceful eighteenth-century houses, many of them turned into offices for professional men such as solicitors and accountants.

Angus nodded feebly at a Queen Anne house, one Kate had admired often. It was colour-washed in palest green and roofed with hand-carved terracotta tiles. There was no front garden; the oak door opened on to the narrow pavement.

Kate was helping Angus out of the car when the door opened and a woman appeared. She couldn't be Angus's wife, unless he had married someone considerably older than himself, and Kate doubted whether she was the housekeeper, the way she began at once to scold. His sister obviously, her hair was the same gingery-red colour.

She had a soft Highland accent which Angus lacked, and though she berated her brother, her voice was full of concern and her grey eyes anxious.

Between them the two women got Angus into the house and through to a room that overlooked the garden at the back. He collapsed on to the settee. 'Get my chloroquine,' he gasped.

Though Miss McGill was heavily built like her brother she was quick and light on her feet. In seconds she had returned with the tablets. 'Perhaps you'll take more notice of me in future!' she reproached him.

'Stop your blethering, woman, and help me to bed.'

'Can I be of help?' asked Kate.

Miss McGill gave her a kindly smile. 'That's very kind of you, my dear, but I think you've done your share of hoisting my hefty brother about. You sit yourself down and have a rest. I'm used to this, I've had enough practice.'

Kate was glad for a chance to sit, she still felt shaky in the legs. Angus's condition shocked her, it wasn't often she saw a man with his reserve of strength suddenly become as weak as a kitten. In a short time his sister reappeared.

'Well, well, the poor man might sleep now and let's hope he'll wake up feeling better. I warned him not to go to that wedding. He'd been working out in the garden all morning and didn't leave himself enough time to change, typical of Angus. I guessed he was due for another bout of malaria, he's woken up these past three mornings with his pyjamas drenched in perspiration—ague, my dear, a sure sign. He assures me the malaria will burn itself out in time—he's usually right. Not that I would give him the satisfaction of admitting that. He's bigheaded and pigheaded enough as it is!'

Kate warmed to Miss McGill.

'I'm Alice, my dear,' she said, introducing herself. 'And Angus said you were Dr Murray—another good old Scottish name.'

'Away in the past, I'm afraid,' Kate was quick to inform her. 'The Murrays have lived in London for generations. And please call me Kate, your brother does.'

'And without your permission, no doubt, if I know Angus! Still, I'm glad he's back from Africa— I missed him. I grumble about my young brother, but I wouldn't be without him.'

'I have a younger brother too, so I know what you mean,' said Kate, and the other woman beamed.

'Well then, so we have something in common. My dear, I hope this means we'll be friends and that you will come to visit me often. Will you stop and have a bite of supper?'

Kate had half a mind to accept. She was tired and hungry and having someone to talk to would take her mind off Martin—and the sitting-room was so pleasant, tastefully decorated with a view over a large informal garden at present lush with roses. But—and it was a large but—there was also Angus, and he might appear again as soon as the chloroquine had taken effect. She had had quite enough of Angus McGill for one day. She rose.

'Thank you, but I must get back—I'm on call from seven o'clock. I hope your brother will soon recover.' It was a remark made in politeness more than concern. As Alice McGill walked her to the front door, a voice bellowed hoarsely from upstairs:

'Alice, what in the hell have you done with my other green shirt?'

'He's obviously feeling better,' said Miss McGill fondly.

CHAPTER TWO

YELVERTHORPE looked its best in the early evening light when the sun was low on the horizon, and the cobbled square free of traffic. In the leaning sunlight the old granite buildings had a mellowed look, and the River Yelver, glinting with silvered ripples, made its placid way towards the ravine at the lower end of the town.

The town had grown up around the river in the latter part of the eighteenth century, when wealthy merchants from the industrial area had moved out to more congenial surroundings. Now sheep grazed on the surrounding moors and in the summer were joined by the black-banded Galloway cattle, a breed recently introduced.

Here in Yelverthorpe, time gave the appearance of standing still. The inhabitants went unhurriedly about their business. A newly constructed bypass had brought a reprieve from noise which only burst out again on market days when all the roads radiating from the square were jammed with cars and delivery vans, but that was accepted as part of an old tradition. There had been a market in Yelverthorpe for two hundred years.

But appearances were deceptive, as Kate discovered within a few weeks of taking up her appointment as assistant at the group practice. Beneath that leisurely exterior life was thrusting and competitive. It was a prosperous town with many good shops, and its nearness to an attractive coastline brought in the holidaymakers.

Tourism wasn't its main industry, however. A new trading estate had been built on the outskirts of the town and supported many successful small businesses. If Kate had expected an easy time in general practice there she soon found out differently—not that she minded. It was because of her addiction to work that she had qualified at twenty-two, the youngest age possible.

After qualifying she had spent nearly three years in hospital work hoping to specialise in medicine, but competition was keen, and until she reached the status of a senior registrar her salary would have been insufficient to cover living expenses for herself and Simon.

General practice was the answer, and she began to study the adverts in the *British Medical Journal*. She hadn't intended to go far afield, but nothing suitable came up nearer home. In answer to one advertisement she wrote to the senior partner of the Yelverthorpe group practice, a Dr Barnes.

His answer was encouraging. He was impressed with her record, but he really wanted an assistant with some experience of anaesthetics. Of his two junior partners, Dr Audrey Pettifer had a diploma in gynaecology and obstetrics, and Dr Derek Lambert in paediatrics. The day of the old family doctor was fast disappearing, Dr Barnes' letter explained, group practices were now *ipso facto*, and GPs were expected to have specialised knowledge of other branches of medicine. Would she consider studying for a diploma in anaesthetics? As for himself, he was nearing retirement age and mostly

confined his work to the administrative side of the
practice. Would she come and see him?

Kate did, driving herself the hundred and ninety-
odd miles to Yorkshire and arriving on a crisp April
afternoon when the wind was as sharp as cold steel.

She had stopped the car on a ridge overlooking
the town. It was market day, the colourful striped
awnings belonging to the stalls contrasted vividly
with the sombre stone buildings that enclosed the
square. The river, from a distance, looked like a
wide grey moving strand that threaded its way
through clusters of houses and shops before
disappearing out of sight in the gorge. At its widest
point it was spanned by an immense brick-piered
railway bridge, defunct since trains no longer ran
through the town, but retained as an example of
the best of Victorian industrial architecture.

Stretching up as far as the eye could see was
moorland, brown with last year's growth of heather—
studded with trees not yet bursting into new
life, ribboned with winding stone walls—to many
sightseers bleak and forbidding. For Kate the wild
landscape held an instant appeal, and from that
moment her love affair with Yelverthorpe began.

Dr Barnes was a small, fastidious little man, fussy
in speech and manner, but under that manner was a
shrewd business sense and a quick perception of
others' capabilities. He sized Kate up at once and
offered her the assistantship with a view to a
partnership but with one proviso—that she would
take a diploma in anaesthetics. This she did within
two years, studying during her leisure hours. Now,
as well as her general duties she did two sessions a
week as an anaesthetist at the District Hospital and
helped out whenever she was needed at the Cottage
Hospital.

She had lived for a time with Audrey Pettifer and her husband, a local schoolteacher, until she had found a home of her own. Now she was renting one of the small stone cottages that overlooked the river near the bridge. In the nineteenth century they had been artisans' homes, now they were looked upon as desirable residences, especially by young professional newlyweds. Kate was lucky to find one to rent—the owner lived in Leeds and let it as a holiday cottage, but as he was going abroad for three years had agreed to a long lease.

It was furnished after a fashion, and Kate had added her own little touches. The rooms were small and the kitchen gave her the shudders, but she could lie in bed and listen to the ceaseless lilt of the river and see the trees on the opposite bank climbing up the hill to where the stone tower of a church broke into the skyline.

Simon, who had moved from Snaresbrook into a hostel, spent his holidays with her, and Martin came the odd weekend, though he wouldn't stay in the cottage, knowing it might bring Kate into disrepute with Dr Barnes. His last visit had been at Christmas and he had stayed as usual at the Black Lion, and on Christmas Eve they had gone to that fateful dinner-dance at the Town Hall.

Kate was thinking of that now as she left her car in its parking lot at the back of the cottages and let herself in through the back door. As usual Pesky ran to greet her, yelping with excitement, acting as if he hadn't seen her for a month, hopping around her until she picked him up and calmed him with a hug. She had to go through this ritual every time she went out, even if it was only to post a letter. She never thought she would ever behave so sillily over a dog, and a Pekinese at that, but she couldn't

imagine her life without Pesky now. He filled her
need to care for someone.

She flopped down in a chair with the dog on her
lap, unheeding the red-gold hairs he was strewing
about her new dress. She was past caring about the
dress—it had served its purpose, now she never
wanted to see it again. It would only remind her of
the day she had reached the lowest point of her
despair and somehow had survived. Once, in the
church, when Martin had placed the ring on Sandra's
finger, she had wanted to die—just to escape the
intolerable ache in her heart. Unfortunately, one
can't die at will.

What had attracted Martin to Sandra? Kate had
asked herself that times out of number these past
six months. Not money alone, surely? Sandra was
young, only twenty-two, and very attractive, but
she was also vain and utterly selfish. Her two main
interests in life were clothes and herself; Martin's
were widespread; music, sport, reading, talking—
talking above all, and on a variety of subjects.
What had the two of them in common except sexual
attraction, and that could easily burn itself out—
what then? Would Martin come fawning back to his
old love?

The very idea jerked Kate into action. She
jumped to her feet so quickly she dislodged the
snoozing Pesky who awoke on the floor with a
start. The one thing Kate could not tolerate was the
thought of Martin crawling back to her as if she
were a second-best prize—a mere compensation.
Such a thought drove her to the kitchen—anything
to keep occupied, and Pesky trailed after her,
fanning his tail with expectation.

Kate was hungry but was in no mood to bother
with a proper meal. She made herself some peanut

butter sandwiches and switched on the coffee pot; while it was heating she opened a tin for Pesky.

She looked down at him now as he sat up in the begging position looking up at her with eyes full of love and trust. In ancient China Pekinese had been known as lion dogs, and lion-hearted Pesky certainly was. He was fearless, loyal, and a faithful little companion. She had always thought that Pekineses were snappy, bad-tempered little dogs, but she had soon found out how wrong she had been the night she was called out to see Mrs Cotter.

It was a wet, stormy night soon after Kate had moved to No. 9 Riverside Terrace. Mrs Cotter was really Dr Lambert's patient, but he himself had gone down suddenly with 'flu; there was a minor epidemic of it in Yelverthorpe at the time.

Kate soon diagnosed Mrs Cotter as another victim. She was a broad-chested woman, prone to bronchitis, and because of the risk of influenzal pneumonia Kate started her on antibiotics at once. Bed rest, plenty of liquids, and a soft diet in proteins, Kate told Mrs Cotter's daughter who lived with her.

The two women were in partnership together, running a breeding kennels of toy dogs. Pekineses were obviously their favourites; three lived in the house with them as pets, and one was Sukey, Pesky's mother.

Pesky had been a tiny ball of golden-red fluff when Kate first knew him, a sturdy independent little dog who flung himself at her like a golden missile whenever she called. He yapped, certainly, but as Mrs Cotter told her, 'That's one of the advantages of owning a Peke. Houses with Pekes in them never get burgled.'

That wasn't the reason Kate had bought him, she

couldn't believe any self-respecting burglar would waste his time breaking into her humble home. No, in spite of her built-in prejudices against toy dogs, little Pesky had wormed his way into her heart, and she knew she had prolonged her visits to Mrs Cotter long after she had recovered from influenza just to see him again.

'You won't regret buying him,' said Mrs Cotter, as she handed over Pesky for the last time. 'You've got yourself a friend for life—well, for fifteen years of it, anyway. Now, remember what I said, any problems get in touch with me at once, but if you come up against serious trouble contact Havers and Wiles, the vets in Market Street. They're a father and daughter team and very good.'

So it was Pesky who introduced Kate to Rachel, one of the best of the many good turns he did her. She had taken him to Rachel for his initial inoculation.

'There, not a whimper from him,' said Rachel when it was all over. 'A plucky little thing. I bet he's one of Mrs Cotter's. Here you are, back to your mistress, and take good care of her.'

'He's the boss,' said Kate. 'I try not to spoil him, but he's so adorable it's hard not to. As long as he doesn't grow up snappy.'

'Only a snappy owner has a snappy dog,' said Rachel firmly. 'Pets are like children—they learn by example. Somehow, I don't think Pesky will grow up bad-tempered.'

Kate laughed. 'You don't know me yet!'

'I'm hoping to, I've heard a lot about you,' Rachel answered warmly.

Their friendship developed from then on. Rachel was nearer Kate's age than either the Pettifers or the Lamberts, who were all in their late forties. Rachel was thirty-two.

She lived with her small son over the practice in Market Street, in a detached Georgian house. Her widowed father had moved to a modern bungalow on the outskirts of the town near the golf course; he looked after the large animals—the sheep and the cattle and the horses. Rachel saw to the pets and they came in all shapes and sizes, but dogs and cats still headed the popularity poll.

Kate fed Pesky, then took her sandwiches and coffee back to the front room, she had an hour before evening surgery. Unexpectedly, the doorbell rang. With some reluctance Kate went to answer it, but her face lit up when she saw who it was.

'Rachel, I was just thinking of you,' she said. 'Come in, I need cheering up.'

Rachel like Kate was still in her wedding finery, though her buttonhole was beginning to wilt. She took off her hat and hung it on a peg in the hall, then shook out her mop of thick black hair.

'That's better,' she said, following Kate to the sitting-room. 'I'll never get used to wearing hats. I read the other day that hatpins are coming in again. What next—whalebone corsets!'

'You won't have to worry, you're beautifully slim.' Kate envied her friend her narrow hips and slender shoulders. Not that she wasn't slim herself; she could get into a size twelve skirt with comfort, but she had to watch what she ate, whereas Rachel could eat anything and did, and it didn't make an ounce of difference. Kate offered her one of her sandwiches.

'No, thank you, I couldn't eat a thing, I made a pig of myself at the reception. What about you?'

'I wasn't hungry then,' said Kate bleakly.

Rachel gave her a shrewd look.

'I came over to see if you wanted company tonight. I was going to ask you at the Barkers', but you'd disappeared. I felt you wouldn't want to be on your own, not tonight, so I've sent Benjy to Dad's and I'm going to stay here with you.'

For the first time that day Kate felt her eyes sting with tears. Kindness had moved her where despair and an unbelievable yearning had left her dry-eyed.

'That is good of you, Rachel—but I'm taking the clinic tonight. There won't be much work—there never is on a Saturday, but at least it will help take my mind off—well, it'll keep me occupied.'

'And I'll be waiting here with some supper for you when you come back. Then we can talk or watch TV or do anything you like—'

'There's a good film on tonight,' said Kate, dodging the question. She didn't want to talk about Martin—not just yet anyway—not until she was in complete control of her feelings, and she had a long way to go before achieving that.

Later she found she had been a little previous saying that there was never much doing at a Saturday clinic. When she let herself into the surgery, Marie the duty receptionist held up six fingers, at the same time nodding towards the waiting-room.

'You mean six *patients* waiting!' exclaimed Kate.

'Yes—and one has three children with her.'

Kate looked resigned. 'Put some coffee on, Marie,' she said. Coffee was her mainstay when she was tired or downhearted. It had helped her keep awake when she was studying for exams. She knew it was a drug and that she used it as other students used cigarettes, but she wasn't strong-willed enough to give it up—not even when she became a vegetarian and tried to live wholly on health foods.

She was glad of that coffee later that evening. It had been a gruelling session, in just over one hour she had seen a greater variety of cases than she had seen during the past twenty-four hours.

Her first patient was Yvonne Drake, a young woman three months pregnant. What was she doing here on a Saturday evening? Her problems were covered by the ante-natal clinic run by the Cottage Hospital. Kate feared the worst, but soon discovered it was nothing serious.

'Is pickled cabbage bad for me?' the girl asked breathlessly, her thin colourless face puckered with anxiety. 'My gran's staying with me for a few days and she says I'll do my baby harm because I have this craving for pickled cabbage. She says vinegar will dry up my blood, and upset the baby's digestion for life. I don't usually take notice of old wives's tales, not that my gran is that old, but she goes on about it so I couldn't sleep last night, and I suddenly decided to come and see you this evening.'

Kate noticed that the girl's fingers were stained with nicotine.

'Pickled cabbage won't do you any harm, not if eaten in moderation. But you have a diet sheet, haven't you? Pregnant women require additional protein, and I don't think there's much protein in cabbage, pickled or otherwise. Two glasses of milk a day would be better for you and the baby, skimmed milk preferably. What does your gran say about your smoking?'

The girl's eyes widened. 'She smokes a lot more than I do! She's just come back from Jersey loaded with duty-free cigarettes, and she gave half to me. She's very generous.'

Kate kept her opinion of Gran's generosity to herself.

'Weren't you told about the dangers of smoking at the ante-natal clinic?' she asked cautiously. 'Records have shown that there are more fatalities among babies born to mothers who smoke than to non-smokers.'

The girl assumed a mulish expression—this was something she didn't want to hear. She got up.

'It's all right, then, about me eating the pickled cabbage,' she said, avoiding Kate's eye.

'As I said, in moderation, but you'll get over this craving shortly. Just remember to go by your diet sheet and try to avoid spicy and fatty foods.'

The next patient was a man in his fifties. Kate noticed at once that the iris of his right eye was swollen and muddy-looking, and that the upper eyelid was also swollen.

'I think I got summat in't eye, Doctor,' he said.

Kate examined it carefully with her ophthalmoscope.

'When did you first notice the pain in your eye?' she asked.

'I think it were when I went oot wi' lads from the Guild the back end of last week. Must 'ave got summat in m'eye then. I 'aven't been able to see much wi' it just lately.'

Kate examined it again before she gave her opinion. 'You haven't got anything in your eye, Mr Bates, you've got an inflammation of the iris. Why didn't you come and see us as soon as you noticed it, we could have started treatment sooner.'

'I didna' want to worry you abaht a little thing like summat in't eye. I wouldna' 'ave cum now, but me missus got on t' me. Is it bad?'

'You have iritis, and it's very painful, I don't

have to tell you that. I can give you some ointment for it now, but I want you to go to the hospital for a check-up. I'll phone the eye clinic first thing Monday morning and make an appointment for you. They'll put you on a course of antibiotics which will clear up the inflammation, but they'll want to exclude possible complications as well.' Kate gave him a sample tube of atropine ointment, and Mr Bates went off like a man reprieved. Obviously, for him, a visit to the surgery was more of an ordeal than the complaint that took him there.

Next was a young man about Simon's age, and he looked like a student too. He also looked extremely unwell.

'I think I've got glandular fever,' he said, listlessly lowering himself on to the chair.

Kate smiled. She wasn't one of those doctors who objected to her patients diagnosing their own illnesses.

'What makes you believe that?'

'Because I've got all the symptoms—a bit of a fever, headache, and a sore throat. I've also got some funny lumps under my jaw, and I feel so bloody rough. Sorry, Doctor—'

Kate went over to him and gently ran her fingers over his throat. There was no need to take his temperature, his rapid pulse confirmed it was high. 'I think your diagnosis is right,' she said. 'Was it a guess on your part?'

'No, my older brother had it last year. He was ill for three months. Three months feeling like this—God!'

'You won't be feeling like this for three months, though you won't be feeling exactly one hundred per cent either,' Kate told him. 'You've got the long vacation ahead of you, I gather. Yes? Well, there's your chance to take things easy. There's no treatment for glandular fever—we can only treat each symptom, and I can give you something for your fever and the sore throat. I can assure you the disease is never fatal and you'll make a complete recovery. But you must treat yourself as an invalid until you *have* recovered—no undue exertions for the next few months.'

'Bloody hell!—sorry, Doctor—'

He was such a tall, gangling youth and looked so unhappy, he reminded her more than ever of Simon when he was feeling sorry for himself. She put on a teasing schoolmarmish expression.

'And I'll make a pact with you. You stop swearing and I'll stop expecting you to apologise.'

He grinned sheepishly. 'You sound just like my girl-friend! Those exertions you were talking about— does that mean no—you know—' then he stopped, looking at her for help.

'That's entirely up to you. If it's any guide-line I know someone who got married before he'd recovered from glandular fever. It didn't seem to do him any harm.'

His face cleared. 'Thanks, Doc, that news is the best tonic of all.'

The next three patients were more routine. The woman with the three small boys came from a notorious area of Yelverthorpe. It had been condemned by the local council and was due for demolition; in the meantime squatters had taken over the houses in what had once been a respectable working-class street.

The original squatters had been a good class of people, students not able to find accommodation within their means and young married couples unable to keep up their mortgage repayments. They had repainted the old neglected houses and planted out the gardens and it had become almost a self-supporting community. But the idyll didn't last. Drifters and drug-takers joined them; when the houses were all occupied, old vans and caravans were parked in the street and served as makeshift homes. The place began to get a bad name.

Mrs Lee looked like a down-and-out, but her children though dirty were well fed and beautiful—all boys with enormous black eyes. The youngest had mumps.

'You know his brothers are likely to get it too—you should have isolated him,' said Kate, knowing at the same time she was wasting her breath.

The woman shrugged cheerfully. 'I couldn't, could I, there ain't room in the van. Anyway, I 'eard it's a good thing for boys to get mumps early. Saves 'em getting any complications later.'

Kate sighed. It would be wasting her breath even more to point out to Mrs Lee that she had risked infecting the other patients in the waiting-room. Instead she gave her a prescription for a mouth-wash and instructions about keeping the boys away from other children, and in bed if possible, all likely to be ignored. Mrs Lee went away satisfied. She had done her duty, she had taken her children to the doctor's.

The next was an elderly man who had sprained his back while playing bowls that afternoon. It was painful, but after Kate had satisfied herself that no ligaments had been torn and that there was no danger of a slipped disc it was just a question of reassuring the patient and advising him to rest, preferably on a hard flat mattress, until the pain had subsided.

The last patient, and how thankful Kate was to
know it was the last—fatigue was creeping over
her—was a visitor to the town, a holidaymaker. She
had arthritis in one knee and could only walk with
the aid of a stick, she told Kate. Unfortunately she
had left her stick on the coach after a morning tour
of the Dales. Could the doctor please supply her
with another one?

'How have you managed since this morning,
then?' asked Kate.

'I can get around, but it's easier with a stick. I
did phone up the coach office as soon as I discovered
I hadn't got my stick, but they weren't very helpful.'
The woman was touchy on the subject; Kate could
tell she was ready to blame anyone but herself for
her loss.

'I believe there are shops in the market-place that
sell walking sticks,' she said.

This woman didn't like that suggestion one bit. 'I
got that stick on the National Health and I want it
replaced by the National Health! That's what I pay
income tax for!'

Kate sighed. 'I'm afraid—er—I didn't catch your
name? Mrs Moss, thank you. I said I'm afraid we
don't keep walking-sticks in the surgery. You may
be able to get one on loan from the physiotherapy
department of the local hospital, but you'll have to
wait until Monday morning. Would you like me to
write out a chit, or phone the hospital for you?'

'Monday morning will be too late,' snapped Mrs
Moss. 'I'm going home Monday.' She walked to the
door, then hesitated. 'Where did you say I could
buy a stick?'

'The newsagents in the square stocks them and
they keep open until eight o'clock. You'll just make
it.'

'Thanks very much!' Mrs Moss drew herself up, and glared balefully at Kate. 'And I intend to send the receipt to the District Health office and demand a refund.'

'Yes, you do that,' answered Kate.

When Mrs Moss had gone, slamming the door behind her, Kate slumped back in her chair feeling weak and weary. What a day it had been—one she never wanted to experience again. The wedding and all that meant, and on top of that a busy surgery. Fortunately, patients like Mrs Moss were few and far between.

She straightened up as the door opened again. It was Marie, looking surprised and amused at the same time. 'There's one more patient who's just come in. I think you'd better see him—he isn't going to go away.'

Kate exclaimed impatiently, 'Does he know what time it is? We should have shut up shop half and hour ago.'

'I know the time well enough,' a voice boomed from behind the half-open door. 'Time you were home with your feet up!'

Marie's eyebrows shot up to her hairline. Suppressing a giggle, she disappeared, and Angus McGill came into the room. There was a lively gleam in his dark eyes, but otherwise he didn't look well. He was pale under his tan and the excessive sweating of the afternoon had given his cheeks a hollow look. Yet he still managed to achieve that appearance of virile masculinity that would have made his presence noticeable anywhere.

'You should be in bed,' Kate said half-fearfully.

'So should you, but we won't go into that. I don't think I thanked you properly for bringing me home. You missed most of the reception because of me.

The least I can do is take you out to dinner. I've come to ask you to be my guest this evening.'

He had changed into a gingery-coloured jacket that went well with his green shirt but not with his hair. Kate had a sudden overwhelming urge to accept his invitation, then told herself she must be mad. The last thing she needed tonight was the companionship of this ebullient stranger.

'Thank you,' she said primly, 'but I have supper waiting for me at home.'

'Two lettuce leaves and a tomato, no doubt.' He treated her to one of his wolfish grins. 'Come along, girlie, do yourself a good turn. Come and have a steak at the Black Lion. It will put new life into you.'

'I find your invitation difficult to refuse. It will be a real sacrifice to say no,' Kate retorted sarcastically.

His grin widened. 'As one crank to another—'

'I object to being called a crank!'

'OK, Doc. Then as one redhead to another—'

Involuntarily she put her hand to her hair. It *had* been red when she was a child, now she liked to think of it as deep auburn. She was a bit touchy about its colour, having been teased about it so much at school—being called Ginger and Carrots, among other things. 'I'm not a redhead,' she said hotly.

'Stop acting like one, then, and say you'll come out with me.'

She was emotionally and physically exhausted—she was up to her back teeth with men—and that went equally for Martin as well as for this intolerable, overbearing Scot. She leaned forward and stared at him with eyes that sparked off green danger signals.

'For the last time— *no* !' she snapped between

gritted teeth. 'Do I have to spell it out for you? I have no intention of going out with you ever! I'll go even further—I have no intention of ever seeing you again!'

He gave her a whimsical smile, then he straightened his shoulders and with a show of nonchalance put his hands into his pockets.

'Is that so, lassie? Well, for your information, I've been making some enquiries about you. Aye, I haven't wasted any time since I got over my ague—I phoned around. I've discovered you give anaesthetics at the District Hospital, so I've booked you for my next operating session. That's on Tuesday morning. See you then, Doc!' And off he went, leaving Kate speechless.

CHAPTER THREE

CONTRARY to her expectations, Kate slept well that night—that was until the fateful hour of three a.m., when all the gnawing heartache and anguish crowded in upon her again, banishing the prospect of further sleep.

It was not yet daylight, but the waning moon suffused the room with borrowed light, draining colour from the furnishings and sharpening the shadows. Kate stretched out—trying the relaxation she had learnt at yoga classes—but it didn't work for her this time. Her thoughts would not allow her to relax.

Last evening after leaving the surgery she had driven out of her way to go past The Bays, a large mid-Victorian house on the outskirts of Yelverthorpe. This was to be Martin's future home—one wing of it, anyway. It had been built in the 1860s by a retired industrialist from the West Riding, a rambling red-brick mansion, top-heavy with massive turrets. There was an over-indulgence of wrought-iron work along the front façade, and too many gable windows in the high roof, but age had mellowed the brickwork and the surrounding parkland added a natural grace that the house lacked.

The ornamental bay trees that had been planted one either side of the main entrance had grown into magnificent specimens that had somehow survived two world wars when the Army had taken over the house, and foraging parties with axes had plundered the grounds for timber to augment fuel supplies.

The Bays was now owned by a charitable trust who ran it as a private nursing home, and Des Barker was the Chairman of the Board of Governors. It was his idea to appoint a resident doctor, and he had offered the post to Martin, no doubt being prompted by his daughter. Kate had been horrified when she heard that Martin had accepted.

She could forgive him falling in love with Sandra—that was a human weakness—but to give up a promising career as a surgeon for the fleshpots of Mammon was to her mind on a par with prostitution, and she didn't hesitate to tell him so.

'You have every opportunity to become a renowned surgeon—to give all that up to become Des Barker's lapdog, for the sake of a cushy life—you ought to be ashamed of yourself!' she had screamed at him.

Martin had gone white, and his thin lips had tightened. 'You seem to think my new job isn't worthwhile,' he had answered vehemently. 'You should visit The Bays—see for yourself. There's a lot of good being done there, and I shall be proud to join the staff.'

They were the last words they had exchanged in private—after that chance never gave them the opportunity to be alone again. An added irony was that Kate had to visit the nursing home the following week, as one of her patients had been admitted there. Miss Self had suffered a stroke, and after being in hospital several weeks, had been transferred to The Bays. She had private means.

Kate had to change her mind about the place after that first visit. She had always been a little anti private medicine, but now she had to admit that such places did supply a need that was not always available in National Health hospitals owing to lack of finance. An abundance of staff for one thing, both nurses and orderlies, always on hand to anticipate a patient's needs. But even so she came away feeling more than ever downhearted, and it wasn't entirely due to seeing so many frail old people being spoon-fed or sitting propped up before television sets which they stared at with apathy. She had to admit that a resident doctor would be helpful to both staff and patients—but did it have to be Martin with his fine brain? There was no challenge here for him. What about job satisfaction? didn't that come into it too?

What was the point of lying in bed stewing about it? she asked herself now. Dawn was beginning to nudge aside the moonlight, better to get up and make herself a cup of tea.

Rachel was sleeping in the second bedroom at the back. The third bedroom, which was not much larger than a closet, had been converted into a bathroom some time in the thirties.

Kate made the tea and took it into the front room. She drew back the curtains and a pale grey light seeped through the window. The river was leaden colour—everywhere was grey, matching her mood. She heard Rachel coming downstairs.

'Did I wake you?' Kate asked. 'I tried to be as quiet as possible.'

'No, I was already stirring.' Rachel yawned and stretched. In her short nightie she looked like a teenager. 'I'll pour myself a cup and join you.'

'Does the ache of parting ever stop?' Kate asked later, when both in dressing-gowns and curled up in easy chairs they faced the new day.

'It lessens—with time,' Rachel's eyes dulled over as if Kate's words had aroused unwanted memories.

'The first six months were the worst for me. I couldn't come to terms with the fact that Matt had really walked out on me. It was not knowing where he was—or whether he was still in the country or alive even. I imagined all kinds of things. At least you do know about Martin—he hasn't gone off and left you in some kind of a vacuum.'

'No, he's coming back to Yelverthrope to parade his wife in front of me!' said Kate painfully.

'It's not like you to indulge in self-pity, Kate. I've always admired you as a fighter. Don't give in now—don't give that little wimp of a Sandra the satisfaction of seeing you beaten.'

'I won't, I certainly won't do that,' Kate promised, but with a noted lack of enthusiasm. She dug her bare feet into the thick fur of Pesky's midriff, knowing he loved to be used as a footstool, and the warmth of his body was comforting. He looked at her with swimming eyes, barely awake; he wasn't used to such unearthly hours.

'Does it hurt to talk about Matt?' Kate enquired later.

'No, it helps. Dad won't even discuss him with me, and Benjy doesn't remember him,' said Rachel. 'Oh, Kate, I wouldn't go through those first six months again for anything! I used to wait all day for the phone to ring, hoping each time it did that it was Matt—then I used to wait for the postman, praying for a letter, for a card, anything. I'm still waiting, even after five years. I'm still waiting for that phone call or that letter, though I know in my heart it will never come now.' Rachel shrugged her thin shoulders. She said, with an attempt at levity, 'I expect he's married again by now anyway, perhaps got another family. He'd have realised that Dad would see to it that I obtained a divorce.' She suddenly burst out on a note of passion, 'Sometimes I wish I could have an operation on my brain and have that part which is always thinking of him—remembering him—cut out completely. Only then will I ever get any peace!'

Kate had never seen Rachel like this before, her nerves raw, and shaking as if she were cold. She had always seemed so cool, so casual about her feelings for Matt. But Rachel quickly pulled herself together, the trembling stopped and she even managed a faint ironic smile.

'Sorry about that—I let the mask slip then, didn't I? I usually manage to keep better control over my emotions. I've come to terms, after a fashion with Matt forsaking me, but I can't forget what it did to little Benjy. He was such an unhappy, bewildered little boy at first, I'll never forgive Matt for that.'

What kind of a man is it that walks out on his family? asked Kate savagely of herself—then remembered. It was a man just like her own father.

They didn't talk any more then about either Matt or Martin, but later, over the breakfast-table, Kate did touch on the subject just once when she thanked Rachel for staying the night.

'I was in the pits last night when I got back from the surgery,' she admitted. 'God knows what I would have done if you hadn't been here. Just seeing the light in the window as I drove up was a morale booster, knowing I wouldn't be on my own.'

'What about today? It's Sunday—come and spend it with Dad and me.'

Kate flashed her friend a grateful smile. 'No, I shall be all right now, and I've got today all mapped out. If it's fine this afternoon Pesky and I can go on a picnic.' Pesky heard his name mentioned and jumped up on the alert, Kate patted him absentmindedly. 'I want to go over some of my textbooks on anaesthetics this morning—polish up a few things.'

'Whatever for? You've got you Dip.A—sailed through.'

'It's just that I want to be on the safe side.' Kate mentioned the dreaded session with Angus McGill planned for Tuesday.

Rachel gave a broad grin. 'I'm vastly intrigued— tell me more! I did wonder yesterday, seeing you two sitting at a table together, miles away from anyone else!'

Kate ignored that quip. 'Angus McGill came to the surgery last night and told me he'd booked me as his anaesthetist for an operation on Tuesday morning. That's all I know, and I don't see how I can get out of it.'

'Why should you want to get out of it, Kate?'

'Why shouldn't I? I'm surprised you have to ask me! I thought I made my feelings quite clear about that objectionable man yesterday.'

'You called him a gorilla, I remember, but I put that down to the champagne. I've known Angus some time, and I like him.'

Kate started to say something, but changed her mind. She didn't want to hurt Rachel by making rude remarks about her friends. She said lamely, 'He could have tidied himself up for the wedding. Fancy going to a reception dressed like that!'

'Oh, come off it, Kate, you don't really care two hoots how anyone dresses. You're just using him as a scapegoat for your own feelings.'

'How did he come to be invited anyway?' Kate asked.

'Because Mr Desmond Barker spreads his net wide when he goes fishing, and to catch an eminent oral surgeon like Angus McGill would be a big prize indeed. What surprises me more is that Angus actually turned up. He didn't come to the church, I noticed—knowing him, I suppose it was just a last-minute whim. I dare say he got a lot of mischievous pleasure just putting in an appearance to watch what he would call a poppy show.'

'I don't like him,' said Kate decidedly.

'That won't cause him any loss of sleep. But I bet you something—you may not like him, but after seeing him operate, you'll admire him! I'd put a fiver on it.'

Kate was tempted to take Rachel up on that, but there was something about the conviction in the other's voice that acted as a warning. She refused, and Rachel gave her a smug look.

Sunday morning passed quickly. Kate did the necessary chores like washing-up and making the beds. She was a well-organised person and the house rarely got untidy. There was enough left of the salad Rachel had made the day before to have with eggs for her lunch—she could use the rest of the morning to pore over her textbooks.

It was just after three o'clock when she set off with Pesky for their afternoon outing. She drove through the market square and headed for the Dales. The early morning cloud had dispersed and the sky was brilliant. Kate shut out of her mind the thought of two nearly naked bodies on the beach at Alicante and putting the car into a lower gear she started the long winding climb out of the valley.

Kate parked the car on a grassy ridge overlooking the Glaven Valley. She had been driving for nearly an hour, taking her time, weaving in and out of the Dales villages that in their names still carried the heritage of the Viking invasion of a thousand years before. From where she had parked she could look down on a tiny hamlet where a tight cluster of cottages crowded around a Methodist chapel. The river was narrower here than at Yelverthorpe, narrow enough for stepping stones to link the two wooded banks.

This was a country of sloping meadows and stone walls; of miniature waterfalls and fast-flowing becks; of solid farmsteads that looked as if they had taken root—and of sheep. Wherever one looked there were sheep grazing. It was a softer landscape than the high moors around Yelverthorpe, more colourful too. Sunlight patterned the fields, highlighting the dry-stone walls and sparkling on the falling waters. Here was a good place to picnic.

Kate opened the door of the car and let Pesky out. He had been panting from excitement ever since she cut the engine and now shot out like a cork from a bottle. Off he scampered, sometimes stopping in mid-gallop to sniff at a tree, then on again to find something obnoxious to roll in, his favourite sport until Kate put a stop to it.

She took a folding table and chair out of the boot; she liked to picnic in style, even with only a dog for company. She laid the cloth and lit the Primus stove, then picked up the Sunday supplement she had brought along and settled down to read.

Presently, looking up from her magazine, she saw that Pesky had found a friend—a huge overweight, oatmeal-coloured Clumber spaniel. Kate put down her book with a sigh of annoyance. She didn't like big dogs. She hadn't liked dogs at all until Pesky converted her. It was true his new friend didn't seem to think much of Pesky's advances and was trying to ignore him. He stood immobile in glum silence while Pesky pranced around him yapping excitedly. He had sorrowful eyes and long dewlaps which emphasised his look of permanent gloom; finally he lost patience and rolled the smaller dog over with a swift swipe of one huge paw.

Pesky went berserk. He wasn't used to being treated like that—he'd show this shaggy monster who was boss! He leapt up and getting a good grip on the spaniel's ear attempted to shake him. He tried so hard he ended up swinging like a pendulum.

Kate would have laughed if she hadn't been so concerned for her pet. She hurried over to Pesky's rescue. If the bigger dog got nasty he could make mincemeat of the little Peke. But he had his own method of dealing with yappy little dogs who wouldn't leave him to enjoy his Sunday afternoon stroll in peace. When Pesky, exhausted, let go his grip, the spaniel turned and sat on him. He did it slowly but effectively—Pesky completely disappeared under all that heavy fur, only his hysterical cries of rage marked the spot where he had been.

Kate rushed up and began to beat the spaniel about the head with her magazine. 'Get up—get up, you great overfed bolster!' she shouted in panic. She tried to push him away, but he only turned watery eyes on her and his mouth split open as if he were grinning.

Pesky's cries were growing fainter. Kate grabbed hold of the big dog's collar and tried to pull, but it was like trying to move the Rock of Gibraltar. He didn't even growl, just sat there impassively. Kate kicked him in the flank, and that made as much impression as a fly settling on his tail.

'Do you usually go around kicking harmless dogs?' came the amused tones of someone just behind her.

Kate recognised that voice, it had a deep richness she knew belonged to only one man. She was reluctant to face its owner, but what else could she do? There was no getting out of this encounter.

And there he stood, Angus McGill, in the same old jacket he had worn to the wedding, and the same aggravating smirk on his face.

'You call that savage beast harmless?' she demanded. 'It's sitting on my dog, and if I don't get it off soon poor little Pesky will suffocate!'

The man turned to the spaniel. 'Shandy—heel,' he said quietly, but his tone was sufficient. The spaniel rose, ambled across and stood obediently by his side. Kate stared from one to the other.

'I might have known it was *your* dog,' she said bitterly. 'You've both got the same ungroomed look.' They had other traits in common she wouldn't demean herself to mention—like strength and power and a quiet disdain for others.

'Actually it's my sister's dog—and that I presume is yours. What do you call it?'

There was such laughter in his voice as he stared at Pesky, who having got his second wind was now barking at Shandy from a safe distance, that Kate wilfully misunderstood him.

'I call him a Pekinese. What would you?'

'A yapping scrubbing-brush?' he suggested cheerfully.

The kettle on the Primus began to whistle at that moment, and for the first time Angus appeared to notice the table set for tea. There were sandwiches, a salad, and homemade cakes. He gave a low whistle.

'I came along at the right time,' he remarked.

'Yes, how did you happen to be here—just where I planned to picnic?' Nothing would convince Kate it was mere coincidence.

With disarming candour he answered, 'I saw you rattling through the market place in your old banger, and thought I'd tag along to see where you were heading.'

'So you *were* following me!'

He gave one of his wolfish grins. 'Don't flatter yourself, Doc, I had no ulterior motive—just curiosity; thought you might be out on a case. Anyway, I lost you five miles back—catching up with you again was a pleasant surprise. I usually bring Shandy here for his Sunday exercise. Don't you think you'd better rescue the kettle before it blows its top?'

Kate made the tea, then said diffidently, 'As you're here, you'd better stay and join in.'

'I fully intend to, there's nowhere else around here where tea is laid on so generously. Dare I ask what's in the sandwiches?'

'I'm sorry I didn't think to pack ham or tongue, I wasn't expecting you,' she said sarcastically. 'There's a choice of cheese and lettuce, or egg and Marmite, but you don't have to eat them. It's not compulsory!'

He grinned again. 'The one thing I admire about you so much is your charm, it goes with your hair. It that why you chose a redheaded Peke, to see who could outdo one another in temper? I prefer the sound of *your* voice, though,' he conceded. 'It's lower pitched—more pleasing to the ear than that infernal yapping.'

'Pesky— *shut up!* ' shouted Kate, so exasperated by Angus's irony that she lost her temper, and Pesky, never having been shouted at before, stopped short in mid-bark and crawled under the car for safety. Shandy ambled after and lay down by the back wheel for company.

Angus had a good appetite. He ate more than half the sandwiches and made substantial inroads into the parkin. 'This is very substantial tea for one. Do you always do yourself proud like this?'

Kate answered stiffly, 'I thought Rachel might have come along with Benjy. She knew I'd be here.'

Angus squinted down at the piece of shortbread in his hand, then took a generous bite. 'Rachel is a girl I admire. Pity she ever got entangled with that Matt Wiles, everybody could see he wasn't good enough for her—that he wasn't a stayer. But she wouldn't be told.'

'Perhaps it was the *way* she was told!'

'Was that a dig at me?' Kate could feel his eyes on her and looked away. 'I didn't advise her one way or the other. I don't interfere with other people's lives.'

He really believed it, she could tell that. He had no idea of his steamrollering, domineering manner.

'You don't interfere! You pushed yourself on me at the wedding, you came storming into the surgery last night and ordered me—yes, ordered me to be your anaesthetist on Tuesday, and you don't call that interfering!' She glared at him.

'I'd call that being discriminating.'

'What d'you mean?'

'I picked you out as the most remarkable girl at the wedding, and I was right. Look how you came to my rescue. And as for wanting you to assist me on Tuesday—why not? If *I* think you're good enough, why should *you* worry!'

His arrogance was unbelievable.

'I'm not worrying, but I hope you know I only recently got my Dip.A—'

'I know all about that, I checked on you first. The hospital has a very high opinion of you, and you must admit your track record is impressive. Qualifying at twenty-two! That took some doing.'

It had meant studying when other girls her age were out with boy-friends. It meant sitting at her desk evening after evening with her hands glued to her ears cutting out the noise of television, and passing traffic, and sounds of raised voices in the flat below, while her eyes went fixedly over page after page of text—but it had all been worth it in the end. Simon was getting the benefit of it now. Her expression softened.

'You know you look quite pretty when you smile,' Angus McGill remarked, and Kate came back to the present with a jolt. The man was impossible! She turned her back on him and gave her attention to the two dogs instead.

They were firm friends by now, taking it in turn to chase each other, and though Shandy had put the yapping youngster in his place it was plain to see that Pesky was boss. It was he who took the lead in each new game with the spaniel goodnaturedly following after. In that, he differed from his master, thought Kate, who couldn't imagine Angus McGill acquiescing to anything she suggested.

She took a sneaky look at him now as he lay full-length on the ground beside her. She had the advantage of height as she was perched on the only chair, but it was most uncomfortable. If it weren't for the fact that he might put the wrong interpretation on it she would have joined Angus on the grass.

As she watched he opened his eyes slightly and she saw a gleam of dark blue irises beneath lowered lids, and for some reason her heart fluttered. That annoyed her. She got to her feet and in a brisk manner began to repack the picnic case. Lazily he looked on, making no move to help. He was comfortable lying there, his head pillowed in his arms. She had to step over his legs every time she went to the car.

'What's the hurry?' he drawled in his deep voice.

'Oh, *you* don't have to hurry—you take your time. No doubt your sister will have your evening meal waiting for you on your return—your clothes washed and ironed and ready for wherever you intend to go this evening. I don't have a wife or a sister to wait on me, I have to do everything for myself including getting Pesky's supper, and I'm going home to do that right now!'

Angus raised himself on one elbow. 'Have you ever read *The Taming of the Shrew*?' he asked conversationally.

'At school. Why do you ask?'

'Did you see the film with Taylor and Burton?'

She frowned. 'I don't see the point of this conversation.'

He rose to his feet in one swift movement. She marvelled how so big and clumsy a man, could when he liked, move with such lithe grace.

'The film was a very loose interpretation of the play, but it got its message over just the same—how to tame a nagging woman. Come, kiss me, Kate.'

He grabbed her so swiftly and kissed her so thoroughly she had no chance to resist, but she struggled so much he let her loose. She backed away and glared at him with crimson cheeks, more affronted by his words than his actions.

'How dare you call me a shrew!'

He grinned disarmingly. 'If the hat fits wear it, my dear Kate. But heed my warning. Every time you nag me I'm going to kiss you.'

'You're an insufferable bully, and if this is your idea of a joke, it's in very poor taste,' she said coldly.

He regarded her long and steadily. 'Poor Kate, you really don't know how to unbend, do you? It must be all that burning of midnight oil when you were a student. Take a look at our dogs over there—see how they romp together. They've settled their differences.

Couldn't we follow their example and drop this stupid enmity?'

She might have agreed but for one thing. Even in the midst of protesting she could still feel the warmth of his lips pressed against hers, still feel the surge of pleasure that had rushed over her at being aroused in so masterly a fashion. The sensation hadn't lasted. She was shocked at herself for harbouring the thoughts of being mastered. But the idea persisted, even though she told herself no man would ever be *her* master. She had never considered herself the weaker sex. Why, without her where would Simon be now? And Martin? An inner voice queried, 'Alicante?'— and she wondered with a sudden agonising doubt if it had been her strong sense of self-reliance that had driven Martin away.

Kate came back to the present, conscious that a subtle change have come over Angus's expression. His eyes were thoughtful, the sardonic leer had left his face. He was regarding her keenly and she had the uncomfortable conviction that he could read her mind.

Don't be absurd, she told herself, but knowing at the same time that when her guard was down her face was an open book for all to read. She turned away and slammed the boot of her car shut. 'Pesky!' she shouted without looking round. 'Time to go.'

Pesky came trotting up and she picked him up and bundled him into the car. The presence of Angus waiting for her answer unnerved her, and she had the feeling he knew this and that it amused him.

'Would you mind telling your dog to move? I don't want to hit him when I back out,' she said with exaggerated concern.

Angus called Shandy to heel again, then went up to the car and looked through the open window.

'Do you realise the amount of good emotion you're using up just bickering with me?' he asked. 'Such a pity not to channel it into something more worthwhile, such as trying to like me for a change. I always thought non-meat-eaters were docile. You're the first man-eating vegetarian I've ever met.'

Kate roared off in a cloud of exhaust, and had the satisfaction of hearing him cough. But once on the road, she let herself go and started to laugh. She couldn't help it. Angus McGill was insufferable—he was a boor—but he was anything but dull!

CHAPTER FOUR

MONDAY morning brought a letter from Simon. He had arranged to come up to Yelverthorpe for a short holiday in late June, but Kate had heard nothing from him since this plan was first mooted. She had tried phoning the students' hostel, only to be told he was away for a few days.

Away for a few days—and without telling her! That wasn't like Simon. No good reminding herself he was nearly twenty and a man; to her he was still her young brother and she couldn't help worrying about him.

His letter did nothing to reassure her. It bore a West Country postmark and was so brief it could all have been written on a postcard, *and* he had omitted to put his address. The gist of it was that he was staying for a short while in this old garrison town, had something of importance to tell her, and would be in touch shortly.

Thoughts of this 'something of importance' intruded on her mind all day. She couldn't help feeling that what Simon thought important might turn out to be a disaster—going on past experiences.

Halfway through the morning she was summoned to the phone to speak to someone ringing on behalf of an elderly neighbour.

'Is that you, Dr Murray? It's old Mrs Thorn, she's got something in her eye and it looks right nasty. It happened early this morning and she's only just come to tell me. I think she's been rubbing it and it's all swollen up.'

'I'll be along immediately,' Kate promised. She knew Mrs Thorn, a quiet little old lady who lived on her own and tried not to be a nuisance to anyone. The mere fact that she had gone to a neighbour for help proved there must be something wrong. Kate hoped it wasn't another case of iritis or Dr Barnes would start thinking in terms of an epidemic.

Mrs Thorn lived in an old stone cottage next to the chapel where she had been married more than fifty years before. In her small front garden was a beautiful copper beech with a preservation order on it, and though Kate loved trees and would have hated to see this one cut down she did admit it presented problems. All through the autumn and early winter Mrs Thorn could be seen sweeping up the leaves from the narrow pavement, and the tree itself shut out the light from the front of the cottage. Not that Mrs Thorn was one to complain. She loved her tiny home and wouldn't dream of living anywhere else. 'I've got such quiet neighbours,' she would say with a smile, looking over the fence at the burial ground behind the chapel.

The door of the cottage had been left on the latch, and Kate went straight through into the living-room. Mrs Thorn was sitting by a small fire with her pet cat on her lap. Though it was a sunny day the cottage struck Kate as being cold. The walls were so thick it took ages for any warmth to penetrate.

'And what have you been doing to yourself, Mrs Thorn?' she asked feelingly as she bent to examine the old lady. 'Your neighbour told me you'd got

something in your eye. It's a very nasty something,
by the look of things. Now I want you to look
down—yes, that's right. I won't hurt you, I just
want to take a look under your eyelid.'

Kate took hold of the scant eyelashes in one
hand, and with the other averted the lid. What she
saw made her draw in her breath in silent horror.
Embedded in the inner side of the eyelid was a
piece of glass. Small wonder the eye was so swollen
and bloodshot, but how had this frail old lady come
to do such a thing, and what was more, how long
since it happened?

Deftly and swiftly, Kate removed the glass splinter
and a few drops of blood trickled out of the wound.
She went to the kitchen for warm water, added a
little salt, and returned to bathe the eye. She had
no antiseptic eye-drops with her, but she could
make arrangements for the District Nurse to call
and clean the eye thoroughly and to show Mrs
Thorn how to use an eye-bath. Kate shuddered at
the thought of how narrowly Mrs Thorn had come
to losing the sight of that eye.

And all this time the cat hadn't moved from his
mistress's lap. Purring loudly, he kneaded away at
her skirt, and Kate noticed how Mrs Thorn's thin
veiny hands kept a tight hold of him as if to draw
strength from his nearness.

'There, that's all over with, you should be more
comfortable now,' Kate said cheerfully. 'I'll make
you a cup of tea before I leave, but tell me—how
did you come to get a piece of glass in your eye in
the first place?'

'It flew up when I smashed the aspirin bottle—'

'You *smashed* an aspirin bottle?'

The old lady smiled selfconsciously. 'I had such a
bad headache, Doctor, and I couldn't get the bottle

open. It had one of those granny-proof tops, so I got out my rolling-pin and smashed it. The glass went all over my kitchen floor and so did the aspirins. But I didn't care at that time of the morning.'

'What time was this?'

'About three o'clock it must have been, I think—' Mrs Thorn subsided into silence, stroking her cat and giving a little sigh.

'Mrs Thorn, are you telling me you've had a bit of glass in your eye since three o'clock this morning? My Godfathers!—when I think of what could have happened. You've had a lucky escape, do you realise that?'

Mrs Thorn nodded; she didn't seem at all concerned. Her bad eye was so swollen she could hardly see out of it. The cat continued to purr contentedly. Kate marvelled at the resilience of animals and old ladies.

In the kitchen she found the remains of the 'granny-proof' aspirin bottle in the pedal-bin. These child-proof containers were difficult for the elderly, especially those like Mrs Thorn whose hands were swollen with rheumatism. Kate found the aspirins too, in an egg-cup. Someone had cleaned up the kitchen, no doubt the helpful neighbour. Kate emptied the tablets into one of the phials from her visiting-case and labelled it, then made the tea. She would have liked to have stopped longer than she did, but she had her other patients to think of too.

The Yelverthorpe Health Centre was situated in a side street just off the market square. To reach it Kate had to drive down Market Street where Rachel's practice was, and as she passed the detached Georgian house she saw Rachel coming along with a load of shopping. Kate drew into the kerb.

'Hi,' Rachel greeted her. 'Are you free? Come and have a bite of lunch with me. I've got a granary loaf and some Brie—your favourite.'

It was true, Kate couldn't resist Brie. She parked and followed Rachel through a brick arch and into the cobbled courtyard at the rear of the house. Here, the old stables had been converted into modern boarding accommodation for cats and dogs. The animal surgery was in a big room at the back of the house, the front rooms were used as the office, waiting room, and store-room. Rachel's flat was above, inconveniently large for one young woman and a small boy, but it had gracious high-ceilinged rooms with views of distant moorland beyond the town.

'How's Benjy?' asked Kate, as she helped carry Rachel's shopping into the kitchen.

'Fine. He hasn't had one of his attacks for weeks, so I'm keeping my fingers crossed.'

Benjy suffered from a form of children's asthma. At its worst it was so severe that when Kate had first seen him in an attack she had mistaken it for bronchial pneumonia. Rachel referred to such afflictions as his 'wheezy attacks'. They had started soon after his father left them when Benjy was only three, now the attacks were triggered off by a variety of causes. Allergy was one of the main reasons—allergy to house-dust or feathers, and animal fur (Rachel kept him well away from the surgery). Sometimes his asthma was brought on by some worrying emotion or sometimes just something he had eaten which didn't agree with him. Yet Benjy was a happy and contented little boy. Dr Derek Lambert had told Rachel not to worry unduly about him, that he would grow out of his asthma in time, and if it was any consolation to her the majority of children suffering from this complaint were above the average in intelligence. Rachel didn't say so, but she would have swopped Benjy's intelligence for a clean bill of health any day.

'You look unusually tired, Kate,' she remarked as she poured coffee. 'Had a busy morning?'

Kate told her about Mrs Thorn, and Rachel gave an incredible whistle.

'Don't tell me you were called out to that old dear too! I was up at her cottage at two o'clock this morning.'

'You! What did she want with you?'

Rachel laughed. 'She dragged me out of my sleep to tell me that Toots (Toots, what a name for a cat!) was stuck up in a tree and couldn't get down. My first reaction was to tell her to leave him, that he'd come down of his own accord. I know Toots of old—dear Mrs Thorn must spend half her pension on vet's bills—then it dawned on me that Mrs Thorn isn't on the phone and she must have walked half a mile to a kiosk—and she was crying, I could hear her. How she was crying! Toots had been missing all day Sunday and she hadn't gone to bed because she was so worried about him. Then she had heard this faint miaowing and had traced it to that old copper beech in her front garden. Doubtless some dog had chased the wretched cat up there in the first place and he couldn't get down.'

'She could have sent for the fire brigade.'

'At two o'clock in the morning? Mrs Thorn wouldn't even consider it. But she knew me, she trusted me, so I got dressed and went over.'

Kate gave her friend a look of incredulity. 'And

you *climbed* that enormous tree! How did you get a hold? It's sheer trunk for the first ten feet.'

'I stood on the railings and Mrs Thorn held a torch for me to give me light. I was able to reach the first branch and swing myself up. Coming down was worse as I was clutching Toots with one hand. Look what the ungrateful little beast did to me,' and Rachel showed scratches on her upper arms and neck.

'You might have killed yourself!' exclaimed Kate.

'Well, I didn't, so stop glaring at me like that. Why did you have to see Mrs Thorn?'

It took Kate a little while to marshal her thoughts. She kept thinking of that tree and the ugly spiked railings beneath—and then the injury to Mrs Thorn's eye. How could one sweet-natured white-haired old lady be such a menace?

She explained about the fractured aspirin bottle and Rachel laughed again, but ruefully this time. 'Poor old soul, I suppose all that worry about Toots brought on a headache. But smashing an aspirin bottle with a rolling-pin! She doesn't look as if she had the strength.'

'And you don't look capable of climbing a sixty-foot tree,' retorted Kate.

The rest of the day followed its usual pattern, which was just as well from Kate's point of view as now she kept thinking of the following morning and her session with Angus McGill. She spent most of that evening going over her textbooks again, and got more and more worried as it dawned on her that there was still much she had to learn about anaesthetics. Like Mrs Thorn, she soon had a raging headache, but didn't have to smash the bottle to get to the aspirins. She did think, however, that the powers-that-be could think of some alternative means of keeping tablets safe from children without making it virtually impossible for the elderly and infirm to open the bottles themselves.

The Town Hall clock was striking nine when she turned into the gates of the District Hospital the following morning. She wasn't due until nine-thirty, but she liked to be punctual and wakefulness had got her up earlier than usual.

The hospital was a neo-Gothic Victorian building which had seen many changes in its hundred years' history. It had been upgraded in 1948 when the National Health Service came into force; it was then effectively modernised and over the years extensive alterations had been made to it. The new dental block had only been completed within the past decade. It had its own administration offices, X-ray unit, and orthodontic department, and dental students from different teaching hospitals were a familiar sight in the wards or the common-room. They considered themselves lucky to be sent to Yelverthorpe on a course, thus providing a chance to work with Angus McGill.

Though Kate had been working at the hospital for some months now, this was her first time inside the dental department, and she was agreeably surprised by the appearance of the entrance hall. There were flowers everywhere, so tastefully arranged that it had more a look of a hotel foyer than a hospital. There was a tea bar and a shop and a newspaper kiosk, all run by the local Red Cross, and fitted carpets and easy chairs increased the feeling of being somewhere pleasant and relaxing, and Kate wondered if it had been designed with that idea in mind.

She went through to Reception and said she had

an appointment with Mr McGill, and was sent to the upper floor.

There was a lift, but she preferred to walk up—she had plenty of time, and the first person she met when she came through the door into the corridor was Angus himself.

He greeted her with a smile, showing an expanse of large white teeth. 'That's what I like to see—eagerness to get started!' His strong voice seemed to bounce back off the walls, and Kate winced. She wished he could temper his voice a little. 'Come into my office, Doctor, and I'll put you in the picture.'

Much to Kate's surprise his office was the model of tidiness, and she guessed that was entirely due to the efforts of his secretary. Angus didn't look so scruffy himself this morning either; no doubt the white coat covered a multitude of sins. He sat down at his desk and invited her to sit opposite.

'My first patient is a Mrs Leonard,' he told her. 'Here's her X-ray. Does it mean anything to you?'

Kate studied the film trying to look more knowledgeable than she was actually feeling; the very presence of this man was enough to make her forget all she had ever learnt.

'It's an X-ray of the upper jaw. I can see a shadow. Is it a cyst?'

'Good girl. Yes, it is a cyst—of the superior maxilla. Normally I would deal with it under a local anaesthetic, but Mrs Leonard has a nervous disposition and I don't believe in putting my patients under any more stress than is necessary. Curious case this, really.' He pursed his lips reflectively. 'Mrs Leonard is a woman in her sixties, and about forty years ago during her first pregnancy she developed severe toothache in one of her front

incisors. Her dentist couldn't find anything wrong—
she had good teeth and still has—but because she
kept begging him to do something to ease her pain
he took out the nerve. This successfully killed the
pain, but it also killed the tooth, which became
discoloured and eventually turned black. Mrs
Leonard became very selfconscious about that tooth,
being right in the front it was noticeable every time
she smiled. Anyway, she put up with it for years,
then a short while back she won a Premium Bond
prize—nothing spectacular, but sufficient to pay for
private dental work. She wanted that black tooth
crowned.'

'Couldn't she have got that on the NHS?' Kate
queried.

'Not for cosmetic reasons only. The tooth was
dead and unsightly but hadn't given her any trouble
since the nerve was removed. Anyway, as soon as
her dentist saw the X-ray of the tooth, and the cyst
growing from the root socket, he sent her along to
see me. *Now* Mrs Leonard will get her crown on
the National Health, because it's essential that cyst
is dealt with before it grows any larger.'

Angus rose to his feet and Kate followed suit.
'My other case is quite straightforward—impacted
wisdom teeth—all four of them, and the patient is
one of my own students. So come along, Doctor,
let's get cracking.' His manner of speaking was
brisk but friendly, there was none of his usual
familiarity. He appeared to Kate a more responsible
kind of person, and grudgingly she began to feel a
growing respect for him.

He led the way into the smaller of the two
operating theatres. It seemed full of people; actually
there were only five, but that number was sufficient
to crowd the room. Kate recognised two local

dentists who nodded to her and a young man she took to be a student. There was also a nurse attending to the patient.

Mrs Leonard kept plucking nervously at her gown. Kate went up to her at once and explained what she would have to do—first an intravenous injection in the arm, then when that had taken effect, the general anaesthetic. Mrs Leonard understood and gave a wan smile. As soon as she was unconscious, Kate fixed a band around her upper arm as an aid to check on her blood-pressure and pulse rate during the operation.

Kate didn't see Angus make his first incision, she was too occupied with her own duties, but she heard him explaining what he was doing and why. When she looked up he was removing the diseased bone to reveal the cavity.

'And now, gentlemen,' he was saying, 'it's a question of draining the granulation tissue and then removing the epithelial to prevent it growing again. The cavity will collapse and fill up from the bottom with new bone. It only remains now to close this cavity with the flap and then to stitch the wound. Fortunately, this is not a very large cyst. With a larger cyst I would have inserted a plug, which would have had to be replaced every day, and then the same procedure would follow—the cavity would collapse and fill up again with new bone.' He straightened up and arched his back, stretching himself at the same time. 'That's it then, folks, and I think we can say it went off very satisfactorily.'

At that moment he caught Kate's eye. 'Well done, Doctor!' he bawled cheerfully.

Whether it was the mask that accentuated his eyes or whether Kate hadn't had the chance to study them so closely before, she couldn't be sure, she only knew she was increasingly aware of their extraordinary colour. The irises were such a dark blue they could almost be described as navy, but whoever heard of anyone with navy-blue eyes? It was absurd! But whatever their colour the effect they had on her was electrifying. She couldn't cope with such unexpected feelings at a time like this, and she was glad to turn her attention elsewhere.

She checked Mrs Leonard's blood-pressure and pulse rate for the last time, and satisfied herself that the pupils were reacting normally. Everything was satisfactory on her part too. As soon as Mrs Leonard began to come round Kate knew she could safely leave her in the care of the nurse.

Someone took hold of her arm. It was Angus. 'Come along, time for a quick cup of coffee in my room before the next job.' It was the first time he had given her an order she didn't resent.

The nurse brought in coffee, and told them that Mrs Leonard was now resting in the recovery room. Her husband had phoned to ask if he could take her home that afternoon.

'I'm not so sure about that, I think we'd better play it by ear,' said Angus cautiously. However, he looked pleased at the news of his patient's rapid recovery. He leant back in his chair, clasped his hands behind his head and regarded Kate with some satisfaction. 'Well, now that that's over how do you feel? Wondering why you got so worked up about it? I told you you had nothing to be anxious about.'

Anxiety came in many forms. Yes, she had been anxious about giving an anaesthetic under his watchful eyes, but she had also been anxious about facing him again after that punishing kiss. She was also anxious about the way his nearness affected her; just sitting here facing him made her nervous.

No other man, including Martin, had had such an influence over her, and she mistrusted the feeling of helplessness it gave her.

'I can't claim that I was over-stretched with Mrs Leonard,' she pointed out with a certain degree of primness. 'It wasn't a difficult anaesthetic to administer.'

'Well then, let's see if we can't stretch you a little further with young Mark Holland. All four of his wisdom teeth are impacting the adjacent teeth and pushing them out of shape. I shall have to remove some of the overlying bone, and as the teeth are extra large divide them up into two or three pieces before delivering them through the exit. Fortunately Mark Holland is a healthy young animal, but I think he's going to resent being kept in hospital, he's not used to being a patient. It might be a useful experience for him to know what it's like being on the other side of the fence for a change. He's going to feel very sorry for himself for a day or two, and though I believe I told you it's a straightforward operation, it could be a lengthy one. How do you feel about that?'

Kate had no intention of letting him see her true state of mind. 'I feel more confident now,' she answered with spirit.

Just then Angus stretched his arms and flexed his fingers staring at them with rather an odd expression, and she marvelled afresh at the size and strength of his hands. It seemed impossible that they could cope with such a finicky operation as Mrs Leonard's, and yet they had, and with ease.

On an impulse she asked, 'What made you branch into oral surgery rather than general surgery?'

Nothing seemed to surprise him, not even a question like that out of the blue.

He shrugged goodhumouredly. 'I did a lot of overseas voluntary work when I was a medical student, mostly in Africa. I saw what disease and malnutrition and just sheer neglect could do to the faces of some of the natives, and I wanted to do something to counteract the terrible disfigurement. The other medical teams were doing good jobs— working all hours to save lives, but I felt that having a normal face added another dimension to one's life. And not only to a humble tribesman, but to anybody, whoever they are—wherever they live.' He spread his hands again and stared at them earnestly. 'The good Lord gave me a pair of strong hands,' he went on, 'and I felt it was up to me to make use of them, so when I got my medical degree I went on to qualify in dentistry and then to specialise in oral surgery. Since then I've worked with plastic surgeons on faces that have been grossly disfigured by accident or disease. I've given people new jaws—well, nearly new. Nobody as yet has been able to compete with the original Creator.' He grinned at her, his strong teeth gleaming in his tanned face. 'And here endeth the lesson!'

Oh, why did he have to spoil everything by being facetious, and just when she was hanging on his every word! Why couldn't he be serious just for once! She rose to her feet and pushed back her chair with a touch of impatience.

'I don't know about you, Mr McGill,' she said, 'but I think that as we have another operation due we'd better get started. I have a busy day's work ahead of *me* .'

'Meaning I haven't.' His grin deepened, nothing seemed to offend him either. 'Right, Dr Murray— this way, if you please.'

He led the way to the anaesthetic-room attached

to the main operating theatre, where their patient was waiting. In spite of premedication Mark Holland was still lively enough to chat up the pretty nurse with him, but as soon as he saw Kate he turned his attention to her. Kate had no time for dalliance, especially when on duty, and Mark was injected and out for the count before he even had time to decide whether her eyes were green or bluey-grey.

She followed behind as he was wheeled into the theatre, pulling the trolley that carried the anaesthetic machine, and when he was ready on the operating table put him into deeper unconsciousness. The same young dental student was acting as dresser, and the two dentists, masked and gowned, were also there to watch.

It might have been a straightforward operation from Angus's point of view; but for Kate the first five minutes were the worst. But once she had gone through the usual routine of checking on her patient's pulse and blood pressure, and making sure that there was sufficient oxygen coming through the machine, she allowed herself to relax.

As she watched Angus at work her admiration for him deepened, and she had to be careful she didn't show it, for all through the operation he kept sending her swift glances to see how she was coping, and each time those deep blue eyes met hers she felt her heart leap. By the time the operation was over she felt quite weak, and knew it wasn't entirely due to anxiety over her patient.

After Mark had been wheeled into the recovery room, Angus went off to write up his notes, taking the student with him. The two dentists began a discussion on orthodontics.

Once she had put her equipment away Kate slipped off, unnoticed by the others. She always experienced a release of tension after an operation and liked to be on her own for a while to recover. This time it wasn't to be. Angus came looking for her and caught up with her in the main hospital block where she was queueing for lunch.

'Come along,' he said authoritatively. 'I know a better place to eat.'

Why do I let him? she asked herself as she weakly followed him out of the hospital and across to the car-park. Then she saw his car and remembered with indignation that he had called hers an old banger. And what did he call his own? she wondered. It certainly wasn't new, and was a model unknown to her.

She glared at Angus. 'You called my little car an old banger—so what do you call yours!'

'That, Doctor, is a vintage sports car. By rights it should be in a museum, because they don't know how to create cars like that any longer. It was a beaut in the Thirties—it's priceless now. My students would give their eye-teeth to have such a possession.'

'They need their heads examined!' Kate retorted.

But once they were humming along the unfenced moorland roads she had to concede—to herself, not to Angus—that the car ran like a dream. It was obviously fitted with a new engine, and there was something luxurious about the appearance of real woodwork and real leather and the sight of well-kept brass. Pity Angus McGill didn't take the same pride in his appearance as he did that of his car. She stole a sidelong look at him. He had a well-pronounced chin and the high cheekbones of a Scot, not a handsome man in the strictest sense of the word; some would even think him lowering with those heavy, overhanging brows, but the soft curves of his mouth and the ever-present amusement in the depths of his eyes lent him a certain rugged charm.

Not that he was a charmer to compare with Martin, and at once, thinking of Martin, his image sprang to her mind—the long-lashed liquid black eyes and the handsome classic features. Her whole being ached with longing for him. She clasped her hands in her lap and bowed her head in an effort to stifle the pain that suddenly shot through her. Angus turned sharply to look at her.

'Are you all right?' he asked with concern.

Kate quickly pulled herself together. 'Just a few troubled thoughts—they didn't last. I'm all right now.'

'No reaction from our morning's work?'

'No—no, nothing like that. Something personal—something private.'

'Yes, you are a very private person, Kate,' he said, and she thought she detected a tinge of regret in his voice.

He drew up in front of an isolated moorland inn that looked as if it had seen better days. It had once done a brisk trade serving travellers taking the old drove road across the Pennines. Now it looked unvisited.

'This place used to be noted for its home-cured hams and good strong ale,' said Angus, his eyes gleaming in anticipation of a good meal. 'And not forgetting your tastes—lovely crumbly Wensleydale cheese and home-baked bread to go with it. Or pickled eggs if you prefer.'

Kate followed him into a low-ceilinged, smoky bar-parlour. It didn't have sawdust on the floor or spittoons in the corner, but there was the original old oak settle beside the cavernous fireplace, now empty but for rubbish. Kate looked about with distaste. Angus had brought her away from a clean, modern cafeteria for this!

The place was empty except for one other customer. The landlord gave them no sign of welcome, but went on polishing glasses in a desultory manner. He was a tall, thin man with a balding head and an unhealthy pallor. No wonder, thought Kate, cooped up in this dark hole all day.

Angus went up to the bar, but soon returned. 'Sorry, no ham or homemade bread, there hasn't been any since his wife died, he said. So it will have to be a ploughman's—Hobson's choice. Do you mind?'

'Not at all,' Kate said unconvincingly.

Angus gave her a whimsical look. 'It's kind of you to say so. I expect you think I've brought you here under false pretences. I haven't been here for over two years, and I should have checked first. I'd heard that Mrs Lewis had died, but I didn't know Bob had taken it so hard. He's a mere shadow of himself. You wouldn't believe he used to be the typical ruddy-faced, hail-fellow-well-met kind of landlord?'

'You're right, I wouldn't,' said Kate.

The publican had disappeared into a room behind the bar and was gone so long that she surmised he was making up the lunches himself. The other customer had also ordered a ploughman's. Then the landlord returned with three plates on a tray and morosely handed them round.

Kate looked at the stale bridge roll and the piece of mousetrap cheese, the pickled onion and the tired lettuce leaf, and stifled thoughts of the cauliflower cheese she could have had in the canteen. The lone man at the far table obviously shared her sentiments.

'What d'you call this?' he called across to the landlord.

'Thats a ploughman's,' was the surly reply.

'Humph!—wouldn't get much ploughing done on that,' came from the corner.

The landlord's reaction was swift. He snatched up the plate, slapped it down on the bar, then took some money out of the till and flung it at the dissatisfied customer.

'There's your money back. Now get out of my pub!' he shouted.

The man didn't wait to be told twice. When he reached the door he turned and glared at the publican. 'No wonder ye're losing all your custom, ye miserable awd devil,' he said, and spat on the floor. The door slammed after him.

The landlord turned red-rimmed eyes on Angus and Kate. 'Any complaints?' he asked aggressively.

Angus could have picked him up and wiped the floor with him and Kate expected him to do just that, but instead he answered mildly, 'This will suit us fine, Bob. Just fine.'

'Don't mind me!' Kate muttered.

'Mind you what?'

'I mean I shan't get upset if you want to put that—that tyrant in his place!'

Up went Angus's eyebrows and his eyes darkened in colour as he smiled. 'So you think I was holding back my temper because of you? Kate—Kate, how little you know me! When I do let go, I let go and damn the consequences.' He broke his roll open and buttered it. 'My dear Doctor, I don't pick quarrels with a sick man.'

'Sick?' Kate glanced quickly at the publican who was now slumped down behind the bar with shoulders hunched and his eyes closed. 'He's

unhealthy-looking, but I wouldn't call him sick—
just bad-tempered.'

'Well, putting on my medical hat I would say that
Bob Lewis has a duodenal ulcer. He's got the
typical look of a man in constant pain, and I noticed
that twice he seemed to have a spasm in the region
of the epigastrium. I'd like to have a word with
him, and persuade him to come to hospital for a
check-up—but not now. I'll come back on my own
one evening.'

'I'm the doctor,' said Kate miserably. 'I should
have noticed the signs for myself.'

His smile deepened. 'But I had the advantage
over you. I can remember the old Bob from happier
times. I couldn't believe that the loss of his wife
was entirely the reason for the change in him, so
I've been watching him closely. But I feel I've
cheated you out of a proper lunch. Perhaps you will
let me make it up to you some other time?'

He could be very beguiling when he liked, even
modulate his voice so that the rich baritone tones,
instead of booming out orders, made polite requests
instead. And he was clever at masking the
amusement in his eyes when he wanted to. As a
matter of fact he was such a master of his emotions
that Kate felt at a disadvantage. She couldn't always
successfully hide her own feelings.

'I'll think about it,' she answered cautiously.

She didn't finish work that evening until after
seven o'clock. The lunchtime diversion with Angus
had made her late for her other hospital appoint-
ments and then she had to clear up at the surgery
and do her rounds. Pesky greeted her with more
frenzy than usual when she got home as it was long
past his supper-time. Kate had fed him and was
wondering what she could get for herself when the

phone shrilled. It was her evening on call and she expected a summons, but it was Simon. Her spirits lifted immediately, it was so good to hear his voice.

'When are you coming up to Yelverthorpe?' she asked eagerly.

Simon sounded a little embarrassed. He cleared his throat and gave an unnatural-sounding laugh. 'I'm phoning to let you know I—I mean we—will be up some time next week.'

'What do you mean— *we* ?'

'I'm—I'm married, Kate.'

There was a long silence in which Kate could hear her heart hammering away like a demented clock.

'How can you afford to get married! You're only a student,' she said at last in a voice she didn't recognise as her own.

Again that sheepish chuckle. 'I'm in the Army now, Kate.'

'Are you telling me you've given up medicine!' Her voice rose in a shriek.

'No, I'm telling you that I'm Second Lieutenant Simon Murray of the Royal Army Medical Corps. I've got a cadetship—it's a kind of scholarship. I'll explain when I—that is we, come up.'

Kate felt a sense of bewilderment. It had been a long stressful day and she couldn't take in what Simon was telling her. After a pause she said faintly, 'So I'll see the two of you on Friday, then?'

'Three of us Kate. Lisa is a single parent and she has a little girl of six.'

Shock upon shock. Kate felt too stunned to ask further questions, though without thinking she blurted out, 'Your wife must be a lot older than you are—'

'Only three years, and she doesn't look it. She's a

nurse, Kate. I know you'll like her, and Debbie too. Don't worry—just think how much better off you'll be now. The Army will be responsible for all expenses in future and I'll also be entitled to a second lieutenant's pay. See you Friday.'

Simon rang off in good spirits. Kate could just imagine his relief of having got that off his chest. He was only nineteen, and Lisa was what—twenty-three? A woman of twenty-three is ten times more mature than a youth of nineteen. Kate sat down and wept. Not because Simon had married in this sneaky backhanded manner, but because she suddenly felt redundant. He didn't need her any more.

CHAPTER FIVE

KATE was at the surgery early next morning. Simon's
news had left her in such a shattered frame of mind
that she needed the solace of work to calm her
down.

Three girls were employed at the surgery to do
secretarial work, but Kate preferred to keep her
own records, and she was busy on these when
Audrey Pettifer came into her room.

'What's the matter? Bad news?' asked Audrey
when she saw Kate's unsmiling face. Audrey never
uttered two words when one would do. Some people
found her abrupt manner offputting. Kate had at
first, but several weeks of living under Audrey's
roof when she first came to Yelverthorpe had made
her aware of the caring heart that went side by side
with the analytical mind.

Now she sat on Kate's desk swinging one silk-
stockinged leg. But silk stockings were the only
touch of frivolity about Audrey's appearance—her
hair style was as severe as her tailored suits. 'What
is it?' she asked again. 'What's worrying you, Kate?'

'I had a bombshell from my brother last night.
He told me he'd gone and got himself married!'

Audrey only registered faint surprise. 'Is he old
enough?'

' *I* don't think so. He's hardly twenty and he's
married someone older than himself and she has a

little girl of six. I just can't take it in—it's all happened so quickly and seems unreal.'

The older woman regarded Kate keenly. She had small dark intelligent eyes that missed nothing. 'Are you jealous?'

Kate felt her cheeks go hot. Yes, she was jealous—jealous and angry and concerned—but jealousy was the strongest of her emotions.

She spluttered out excuses. 'If only Simon had told me! It's the sneaky way he went and got married behind my back that gets me—'

'Perhaps he thought you might try and talk him out of it.'

'I would have done too,' Kate retorted hotly. 'Little fool—he doesn't know what he's let himself in for. A family—at his age!'

Audrey slid down from the desk and straightened her skirt. 'I shouldn't take it too much to heart,' she said crisply. 'Who knows, it might turn out for the best. Perhaps Simon will grow up now. I always thought him immature for his age.'

Kate bit back an angry rebuttal. She respected Audrey's judgment and knew she was right. Simon *was* immature for his age. His irresponsible behaviour proved that, but she didn't like hearing someone else say so. She was sensitive to criticism where Simon was concerned.

Seeing the door half-open, Dr Derek Lambert looked in. 'Is this a hen party, or can anyone join in?' He had a jovial manner, quite the reverse of Audrey; he was easy-tempered, voluble, good company. Kate wondered why he had never married, but he was a confirmed bachelor living comfortably with an elderly housekeeper in a tall narrow house in the square. He always said he had never had the time to get married, which could well have been

true considering the number of his interests outside
the practice. Kate looked upon him as a kind of
uncle. She had relied on him a lot when she first
started at the practice and some problems had
seemed frighteningly obscure. She told him of her
misgivings now.

'I shouldn't worry,' he said, which was one of his
typical retorts. Nothing worried him except a patient
who didn't respond to treatment. 'Simon wouldn't
do anything stupid—he's too much like you.'

Complimentary perhaps, but not very reassuring.
Left to herself Kate realised she was not going to
get any helpful advice from her colleagues, and
what good was advice now anyway? Simon was
married—she couldn't undo that.

Her first patient arrived, and from then on she
was kept too busy to think about personal worries.
Late that afternoon she had a call from the District
Hospital asking her if she could come immediately
and help out with some emergency operations.
There had been a road accident and three people
were needing urgent surgery.

Kate looked in on Derek to ask him to see to her
last case, then went off to collect her car and drive
to the hospital. It was a pleasant route once away
from the town, skirting the water-meadows before
the road began to rise towards hilly countryside.
After London where the main hospitals were
situated in densely populated areas, Kate had at
first thought it odd to find Yelverthorpe's hospital
so far out of town, until she remembered it had
started life as an isolation hospital. Isolation
hospital!—she smiled wryly. The words were evocative of nineteenth-century illnesses—of fevers and
infectious diseases. Antibiotics had sounded the
death knell of the old dread fever hospitals; they

had served their purpose once. Now, thank God, they were no longer needed.

An hour later she was walking back from the theatre towards the canteen hoping she wasn't too late for a much-needed cup of tea. The patient she had anaesthetised was a middle-aged woman with a broken collarbone. She had been a front seat passenger in her husband's car and hadn't been wearing her seat-belt. Kate had waited for her to come round from the anaesthetic and checked to see there would be no after-effects, then left her with her husband who, except for shock, had come out of the accident unscathed. The other two victims, a young motor-cyclist and the pillion rider, were both in intensive care.

Kate, lost in thought, almost collided with someone coming round the corner. Two strong hands steadied her and she looked up into a pair of dark blue eyes. Angus McGill grinned.

'Well, well, we're destined to meet, it seems— just when I was thinking about you too. Can you spare a minute?

'I was just going off for a cup of tea.'

'Tea can wait—my patient can't. Come along, it's an interesting case. I'd like you to see it.'

She knew it was useless to protest. He took her firmly by her arm and piloted her out of the main hospital and across to the dental block. She couldn't believe she had been here only yesterday—a whole lifetime seemed to have elapsed since then. Simon's news had distorted reality.

'I hope it's not to give another anaesthetic,' she said. 'You know you should go through the proper channels first.'

'I don't give a damn for the proper channels,' Angus retorted. 'But no, it's not work today—just pleasure. I want you to see what a good job I've made of a very badly fractured jaw.'

Kate sighed. 'It's your modesty I find so endearing,' she said.

Angus steered her in the direction of his dental surgery. 'It's a young lad from Wilberforce Street. Have you heard about that area and its reputation?'

'More than heard. We know all about it, we have patients from there.' Kate was thinking principally of Mrs Lee, the mother of the small boy with mumps. 'How did he come to fracture his jaw?'

'In a punch-up with a much bigger lad. But he's a tough little customer. I had to straighten some of his teeth that had been loosened in the fight and wire up his jaw. I'm taking the wires out this afternoon. He's had nothing but slops through a straw for the past six weeks. I bet he can't wait to get stuck into a juicy steak!'

'Don't you ever think of anything else but steaks!' she cried in exasperation, and he chuckled. 'Often, especially when I come across a nice bit of crackling.'

Kate gave up. She knew she'd never get the last word with Angus McGill.

The boy with the wired jaw was waiting in the dental chair. He was a stocky, belligerent-looking lad, though his eyes lit up when he saw Angus. He was obviously pleased he was going to be freed of the restricting wires that clamped his top and bottom jaws in place. There was no sign of fear or apprehension about him.

Angus went to work swiftly, his nurse handing him the requisite instruments, and the wires were soon removed. Then he made a thorough examination to make sure the bones had been replaced in their correct position and the healing complete before officially discharging his patient.

'And now what?' said Angus, as the boy with a show of indifference shrugged into his jacket. 'I bet the first thing you're going to do is enjoy a square meal!'

The boy squinted at him with baleful eyes, then doubled up his fists. 'Oh, no, it ain't. The first fing I gonna do is find that guy who broke my jaw an' finish the fight. Then I'll fink about gettin' summat to eat.'

'Don't you get disheartened sometimes?' asked Kate when the two of them were alone. The nurse had thrown her a look of despair before escorting the boy off the department. Angus had just stood there shaking with inner laughter.

'I find human nature highly diverting,' he said, giving her a wolfish grin. He looked so tanned and fit it was hard to believe that only four days ago he had been as a weak as a kitten. 'And this time I have a feeling my services will be required on behalf of the other chap.' His amusement faded. 'What is it, Kate? You look as if you have something on your mind.'

'I have, but—' she hesitated.

'It's none of my business, eh?'

'I wasn't going to say that. It's just not important. If you don't mind, I'd like to get back now—'

She walked towards the door, but he put out an arm to bar her way. 'What about a meal together to make up for yesterday? You said you'd think it over. You've had twenty-four hours. I promise I won't mention steak—I'll even take you to a vegetarian restaurant. I couldn't make a bigger sacrifice than that, could I?'

Kate managed to summon up a smile for him. Oh, curse the man for being so persistent—for making it so hard to refuse. She was wondering how to frame her next words when he asked,

'When is your half-day?'

'Not until Friday, and I shall be busy then preparing for my brother and his wife coming for the weekend.' There, she had said it—his wife— perhaps now it would be easier to accept.

Angus looked surprised. 'I didn't know your brother was married. Alice gave me the impression he was still a student.'

'He's only just married. I haven't met his wife yet.'

Her expression, her tone of voice, and the smudges under her eyes told their own story. Her brother's sudden marriage had come as a shock—all the more reason why she needed someone to take her out of herself, reasoned Angus.

'What about next week? Promise me you'll keep your half-day free. I'd like to take you to York. Have you ever been to York?'

She hadn't, she admitted. She had been promising herself a visit ever since coming to Yorkshire, but somehow had never found the time.

'Then it's a must. I know I'm prejudiced, but I think York is the finest city in the North. I'd go further than that—the whole of England.' He smiled. 'You notice I leave out Scotland. That's on a different plane altogether.'

Kate walked back to her car wondering why she had allowed herself to be persuaded so easily. Did she really want to spend one whole afternoon with Angus? Perhaps it wouldn't be such a bad idea after all if it meant that for a few hours she would be free of the spectre of Martin in someone else's arms and the thought of Simon suddenly saddled with a wife and a stepchild.

But even before she drove out of the car park she was regretting the decision. Angus would be able to take her mind off her worries, she had no doubt about that—but at what a cost! She couldn't relax in his presence, all the time she found herself on the defensive. But what made her feel like that? That was what she couldn't fathom out. Why couldn't she accept him as he accepted her—as someone to while away a few hours with, to talk shop, to go places. Oh, if only it could be as simple as that—but there was some chemistry between them that made it impossible.

Friday came, the day she had dreaded. Rachel had been with her the previous evening to help with the preparations. Being Rachel, she neither condemned nor approved of what Simon had done, she just gave practical help when needed. She had brought with her spare crockery and bed-linen, which she knew Kate was short of.

Kate made up her own bed for Simon and Lisa— a four-foot divan, and prepared the single bed in the back bedroom for little Debbie. She herself would sleep in the back room downstairs on the studio couch, a room rarely used because it faced north and was damp.

When the time drew near for their arrival Kate found herself walking up and down the hallway in a state bordering on panic. She was so frightened of showing her disapproval either by voice or manner that she feared she might go overboard in the other direction and appear completely indifferent.

She had had three days to think about the situation and had decided to make the best of things. It was Simon's life, perhaps his whole future—she didn't want to spoil it for him. She had hurried home from the practice and prepared an easy meal, just cold meats and salad, and had changed into a new dress, a pale green linen with white trimming. It was crisp-looking and suited her colouring, bringing out the green tints in her eyes. It also seemed to highlight the red tones in her bronze-gold hair. She knew the girls at the surgery envied her her hair, but perversely she wished it was darker. Something her mother had said when she was a child had impressed on her that redheads were not to be trusted, and she had never been able to dismiss the idea completely. She suspected her father had had red hair.

She heard a car stop outside and ran to the window just in time to see her brother helping a woman and child from a taxi. He paid the driver and the man drove off. How young Simon looked, Kate thought—even younger than his years. He had such a round baby face, and his hair was still as fair as when he had been a child. She saw him give the woman at his side an intimate smile.

Kate had visualised Lisa as a carbon copy of Sandra, perhaps because she saw them both as having stolen from her the men she loved. She had pictured Lisa as someone beautiful and blonde and dressed in the height of fashion, but she couldn't have been more wrong. Simon's wife was wearing a shapeless denim skirt and a plain short-sleeved blouse, and though her face was hidden, Kate got the impression, from what she could see of her, that she was plain rather than pretty.

Putting on a smile that didn't quite reach her eyes, Kate went to the door to greet her guests.

Later that night, lying sleepless on her lumpy couch, Kate thought back over the evening and marvelled that she had survived it with her nerves intact. Lisa had been ill at ease at first, but gradually as the evening wore on and she got over her initial shyness her manner had become more relaxed.

She looked older than twenty-three; if Kate hadn't been told her age she would have put her nearer thirty. She had very pale blue eyes and her lashes were almost white, which gave her face an odd, naked look. She wore no make-up, and her hair looked in need of attention. Kate couldn't help wondering what had attracted Simon to Lisa in the first place. Perhaps she was a scintillating conversationalist—though there was not much evidence of that that first evening.

She did try to make herself helpful, and insisted on washing up after supper. Kate dried up, and as there was only room for two people in the kitchen at one time, this could have been a good opportunity to become better acquainted with her sister-in-law, but the conversation between them was constrained and spasmodic.

'Did you have a good journey?' asked Kate after a longer than usual silence.

'The coach was a bit late starting, but it made up time. We had a taxi from the bus station because it was a bit far for little Debbie to walk.'

Little Debbie, though petite, wasn't as small as she should have been for a six-year-old, Kate thought suspiciously. Had Lisa lied about her daughter's age? The child had her mother's pale blue eyes and mousy hair, and not once during the evening had Kate been able to coax a smile out of her. She clung to Lisa the whole time, only leaving her side when the television was on. She spoke only once during supper, and that was to say she didn't like meat, which made Simon chuckle. He nodded to Kate as much as to say, 'Someone after your own heart!'

Kate had always prided herself that children liked her, she had always got on with them without any difficulty, but she came up against a brick wall with Debbie Stoneham.

Though the child didn't speak much, she put a lot of expression into her eyes, and the glances she threw at Kate from time to time were anything but friendly. It didn't endear her to Debbie either when, after showing her where she was going to sleep, and leaving her a minute to go and fetch a towel, she returned to find the child rummaging through one of the drawers in the dressing-table.

'Are you looking for something?' Kate found herself asking coldly.

Debbie jumped—she hadn't heard Kate return. She turned with crimson cheeks and a defiant look.

'I was looking for somewhere to put my clothes.'

'I've already shown you where to put your clothes—' Kate started to say, but stopped herself in time. Good heavens, Debbie was only a child— what did it matter if a moment's curiosity had got the better of her? Wasn't she, Kate, in danger of venting her disapproval of the mother upon the daughter? Full of contrition, she went down on her knees and gently took hold of Debbie by her shoulders.

'How would you like me to read to you when you're in bed?' she said in a coaxing voice.

'I can read to myself.'

'You can?—and you're only six. You are a clever girl—'

'I'm not six, I'm—' Debbie stopped short and her cheeks reddened again. A trapped look came into her eyes, and she darted a quick glance at the door as if fearful of being overheard. A sudden pity for her stabbed through Kate. A child of this age shouldn't be caught up in the machinations of an adult world. Impulsively, she bent forward and kissed the little girl on her cheek, and swiftly Debbie wiped the kiss away.

When her three guests were in bed, and she was alone downstairs, Kate dialled Rachel's number, half expecting her to be in bed too. But her call was answered immediately.

'Rachel, sorry for calling so late. Would you do me a favour? Could you and Ben come to tea tomorrow? You can!—Oh thank the Lord. You'll help liven things up here.' And events were to prove they did, but not quite in the way Kate intended.

Simon and Lisa and Debbie were out when Rachel and Benjy arrived. Benjy was clutching a tin he wouldn't part with. 'It's something to show your Debbie,' he told Kate in his solemn way. He was a handsome little boy and a combination of large brown eyes and fair curly hair guaranteed him instant admiration. But that hadn't spoilt him. His periodic bouts of ill-health had given him an endurance and toleration beyond his years.

'Where are your guests?' asked Rachel.

'Taking Pesky for a walk. Come into the kitchen, Rachel. I must talk to you.'

'Things are not too good, then,' observed Rachel when Kate had shut the kitchen door after them. Benjy had stayed in the front room.

'I honestly don't know, Rachel. I keep telling myself things could have been worse, that Lisa could have been the *femme fatale* I imagined her. She seems such a harmless little thing, I feel awful having to admit I don't like her—but I don't. She told Simon she was twenty-three and I'm sure she's not a day under twenty-eight—'

'It's not considered a crime for a woman to lie about her age,' Rachel put in dryly.

'It is when the man's a boy and a woman is trying to trap him into marriage. I can't help feeling that she saw Simon as a very profitable meal-ticket and grabbed him. Nurse!—she's no nurse, she's only been training for six months. And she's hard-up for money, I can tell that by her clothes.'

'What about her previous husband? Doesn't he contribute anything?'

'What previous husband? She clams up whenever the conversation gets round to the past. I don't think there ever was a husband, but I wouldn't mind that so much if I thought she could make Simon happy, but I don't see how she can. She'll never be any good for him.'

Rachel was silent for a moment, then she said, choosing her words carefully, 'Have you thought that perhaps it's the other way round? That Simon thinks he might be good for her?'

Kate stared. 'Is that what you think? That marrying this girl is a kind of reaction on Simon's part against my mothering him all these years? He sees himself as being the one doing the looking after for a change! Oh, Rachel—it can't be as simple as that.'

'It could be, but I'll reserve my judgment until I've met the lady in question,' said Rachel. Then, 'Come on, Kate, stop looking like a tragedy queen and help me make some sandwiches.'

Simon had a key to the house and shortly after tea was ready there came the sound of the front door being opened, then the wiping of feet accompanied by a lot of giggling and some excited snuffling from Pesky. Then they all came trooping in, the newlyweds laden with parcels.

'You can see where we've been—to the market! And we've got some fantastic bargains, clothes mostly, and some things for our new flat.' Simon looked flushed and happy. They were all flushed, they must have been hurrying. Kate couldn't help thinking how colour in their cheeks improved the looks of both mother and daughter. She introduced them to Rachel and Benjy, then went off to the kitchen to make tea. Shortly afterwards came a scream of such shrillness that Kate instinctively covered her ears, and Pesky came hurtling into the kitchen like a bat out of hell and tried to hide under the cooker. Kate raced to the living-room to see what had happened.

There she found Simon rolling about on the sofa with laughter, Lisa comforting Debbie, and Rachel and Benjy on their hands and knees searching for something on the floor.

'Whatever happened?' cried Kate.

Simon tried to tell her but couldn't. Lisa said, 'Debbie's just being silly. She's all right now. I'll take her out and give her a glass of water.'

'I'm afraid it's my fault,' said Rachel, getting to her feet. 'I shouldn't have allowed Benjy to bring his new pet here. I didn't foresee the consequences.'

Simon dried his eyes. 'It's only a slow-worm, for heaven's sake! Debbie thought it was a snake and dropped it like a hot brick. Did you ever hear such a loud scream coming from such a small mouth— how did she manage it? Poor Pesky, it frightened the life out of him.'

Nobody was consoling Benjy, who was quietly wiping away tears. Kate got down beside him.

'Have you found your slow-worm?' she asked.

He shook his head. 'And it's so little—it could squeeze down the littlest hole. I only had him yesterday—Grandpa bought him. He's not a snake, Aunty Kate, he's a kind of lizard without legs. I asked your Debbie if she would like to see my pet and she said yes, and then when I put it in her hand she screamed and dropped him. I don't want Pesky to find him, he might chew him up.'

'I don't think Pesky is fit enough to chew anything at the moment,' said Kate, trying not to show her amusement, then she put her hand on something dry and cold that wriggled and just in time bit back a scream of her own. 'Ben!—I think I've found your slow-worm!'

Peace was restored over tea. Lisa was so apologetic it became embarrassing to hear her, but Debbie sat upright on her chair, stony-faced and silent. Kate heard Ben whisper to her, 'I'm sorry I frightened you with my slow-worm. You see, I can't have ordinary pets with fur because they make me wheeze. Slow-worms won't hurt you. They haven't any teeth, so they can't bite.'

But there was no response from Debbie.

This time it was Lisa and Rachel who did the washing-up. Kate could hear them talking away in the kitchen as if they had known each other for years. Could it be motherhood making a bond between them, or was Rachel more charitable in her opinion of Lisa? Later, when Kate saw her out to her car, Rachel said,

'I don't think you have anything to worry about, Kate. Lisa seems genuinely fond of Simon, and he's obviously very much in love with her.'

'Or infatuated,' retorted Kate sourly.

'You'll get over it, my dear. You couldn't have kept Simon in wraps for ever, you know.' Not exactly a remark to endear Rachel to Kate just then.

As Benjy reached up to kiss Kate goodbye he whispered, 'I don't like your Debbie very much.'

'She's not my Debbie, dear.'

'She poked her tongue out at me when I said goodbye. That's not polite, is it?'

No—but quite in character, thought Kate, and gave Benjy an extra hug. Bless him, she felt he was the only one on her side.

It was on Sunday morning that Kate at last had a chance to get Simon on his own. Newspapers weren't delivered on Sundays, so Kate usually collected hers when she took Pesky for his walk. Seeing her getting ready to go out, Simon suggested he went with her. 'You don't mind, do you, Lisa?' he asked.

Lisa didn't mind a bit. She also offered to prepare the vegetables for lunch which they were having early as the London coach left at three o'clock.

It was pleasant walking by the river in the morning sunshine, with Simon more like his old self. It was obvious he welcomed this opportunity for a talk. He explained at some length how he had obtained a cadetship with the RAMC.

He had applied as soon as he knew he had passed his second MB, and had been interviewed by a high-ranking medical officer. He had then been taken on 'familiarisation visits' to a number of Army medical units in order to be shown the career structure in the RAMC.

'Do you think you'll like service life?' asked Kate. She still had her doubts.

'I shall still be a doctor, Kate, that part of my life won't change,' he said simply. 'The other—the social side, the foreign travel—I can look upon as a bonus. And it's up to me to make a go of it as an Army career. For the next three years until I qualify, I'll be paid as a second lieutenant, but there'll be no obligation for me to undertake Army work or take part in military activity during that time. As well as my salary and allowances I'll get an additional book allowance and my tuition fees paid. It's marvellous, Kate, to think I'm truly independent at last!'

She wouldn't let him see the pain his carefree words caused her. She hadn't realised that his dependence on her had become a sore point with him. She said dully,

'And when do you actually take up your duties in the Army?'

'After I've finished my pre-registration year— then I get promotion and, I hope, married quarters. I've only committed myself to a short service commission of six years, but if I like Army life I shall stay on and make a career as an MO.'

'And do you think Lisa will fit in as an officer's wife?'

It was an unnecessary and snobbish thing to say, and Kate was instantly ashamed. She quickly amended it to, 'I mean, do you think she'll like Army life?' But the harm had been done, she could tell that by Simon's expression.

'You have your doubts about Lisa, haven't you?' he said bleakly. 'I've noticed the way you've been looking at her this weekend, as if you didn't know what to make of her. Do try to like her, please, Kate, for my sake.'

She bit her lip. 'Don't you think you're too young to take on a wife and child?'

'Oh, Kate, what has age got to do with it? I'm a man, and now I'm in a position to support a family and make a career for myself at the same time. I thought you'd be proud of me.' His expression suddenly turned ugly. 'Anyway, you're in no position to talk. What about *your* love life—that's been such a huge success, hasn't it! You kept Martin dangling for so long you finally lost him to another woman. What right have you to judge me!'

He strode on ahead, leaving her cringing inwardly, then just as quickly he came running back, and put his arms round her.

'Kate—Kate, I'm sorry—I didn't mean that, please forgive me. I've been so uptight this weekend hoping you and Lisa would get on together. And it hasn't been easy with little Debbie. She resents me—she doesn't want to share her mother with me. I was counting on this weekend helping in some way—bring the three of us closer together, but it hasn't worked out.'

Kate found herself comforting him as she used to when he was a small boy and upset about something. 'Have patience with Debbie, Simon. She'll accept you in time, I'm sure she will—and give me time too.' It was her way of asking for understanding.

She drove them to the bus station when it was time to leave. As she waved goodbye she caught a last glimpse of Debbie staring at her out of the coach window. The peaky little face looked mournful and the eyes had a haunting and lost expression.

Poor little kid, thought Kate, picking up Pesky and carrying him across the cobbled square to the car. Life for a child could be just as fraught with anxiety as for an adult, and it couldn't be easy for Debbie adjusting to a strange man in her life. Her heart ached for both the child and for Simon—and Lisa? But she didn't want to think about Lisa.

As Kate let herself into the house she heard the phone ringing and unsuspectingly went to answer it.

CHAPTER SIX

'HALLO —hallo—' The line wasn't very clear, there was a lot of crackling and disturbance. Then Kate heard someone speak, but couldn't make out who it was. 'Who is that?' she asked, her voice instinctively rising.

There came a long pause, then silence as the interference faded. Next, as clearly as if he were in the same room, she heard Martin say, 'Kate, is that you? Can you hear me?'

Her heart began to race and she felt her mouth going dry. Why was Martin phoning her from Alicante? It could only be because of bad news. Something had happened to him, or perhaps to Sandra. There had been a time when Kate had cursed Sandra from the depth of her heart, but now she was faced with the sudden realisation that revenge was the last thing she wanted. If any harm had come to Sandra, Kate knew it would be on her conscience for evermore.

'Kate! Are you there?' Martin repeated urgently.

'Yes, Martin. What—what's happened—'

'Nothing has happened, you silly girl.' Over the wires came a long-drawn-out sigh. 'I just wanted to hear your voice. I just had to speak to you, that's all.'

Kate's relief was swamped by a sudden rush

of anger. How *could* Martin behave with such irresponsibility?

'Are you mad, calling me all this way just to hear my voice!' she exploded.

Martin began to plead. 'Don't hang up, please, I must speak to you. I'll go insane if I spend another minute in this place! It's all been a mistake—a disaster. This honeymoon—the whole stupid farce of the wedding. If only I could get myself out the this nightmarish mess and come straight back to you—'

This suggestion alarmed Kate, for she knew he was capable of doing just that. She knew too well this side of Martin's character, she had experience of it from the past. In some ways he was like a child who after hankering for a special toy, once having got what he wanted, shows no further interest. But marriage wasn't something to play at—and how could he be tired of Sandra so soon?

There was only one way Kate knew of in dealing with Martin when he was feeling sorry for himself like this. She closed her mind to the longing she had of wanting to shout back at him, 'Come back to me, Martin, leave Sandra. We'll go off together somewhere—we'll start a new life together where nobody will know us.' What would that achieve? A few months of idyllic happiness followed by years of remorse that could destroy them both? Happiness isn't built upon the misery of others. She deliberately hardened her voice.

'For goodness' sake pull yourself together! Good gracious, Martin, you've only been married a week—'

'A few days was sufficient to make me realise our marriage isn't going to work. I had my doubts before the wedding, but I hadn't got the guts to pull out then. To be honest, I was scared stiff of

Des Barker—I knew he wasn't the kind of man to let anyone trifle with his daughter's feelings and get away with it. I've got myself in a trap, Kate, and God knows how I'll get out of it.' Martin sounded even more distraught.

'Not by whining to me,' retorted Kate harshly. She was so near tears she had to appear indifferent or break down altogether. If only Martin had come to his senses before this! Oh, those 'if onlys'. What a burden of misery they concealed!

He didn't answer. She guessed her last retort had struck him like a mortal blow. She said more gently,

'This call must be costing you, Martin.'

'It's not costing me anything but my pride,' he answered bitterly. Then pleadingly, 'Where you're concerned, I have no pride. Help me, darling—I have no one else to turn to.'

That was the trouble. She was his solace—his comforter. Even now, when he was married to another woman, he turned to her as a solution to his problems.

'Listen, Martin,' she said slowly and carefully. 'I've heard before that honeymoons can be difficult, that they're a time of adjustment, and you haven't given yours much of a try yet, have you? I don't want to delve into the past and what we once were to each other—I want to forget all that now, but there are some things we must face up to. We're likely to meet socially and professionally in the future—and we've got to do that like two civilised people. I'll always be your friend, I just can't switch off my feelings for you entirely and I'll always help if you need me—'

Martin broke in with a hollow-sounding laugh. 'In other words, you're offering to be a sister to me!'

Kate hung up. What was the point of carrying on a conversation that was becoming more and more painful to them both? Hunched in a chair, she let the tears run unheeded down her cheeks. Her nerves were already taut from the pressures of the weekend, and Martin's call was the turn of the screw that snapped them altogether.

But her moment of weakness passed, she got to her feet, wiping her eyes with the heel of her palm. Immediately Pesky came out of hiding, crawling appeasingly on his belly towards her. He always took the blame when he saw her upset. With tears still wet on her cheeks, Kate laughed. She swept the little dog into her arms and kissed him. 'You're the faithful one, my Pesky,' she said.

Kate mentioned the phone call to no one, not even Rachel, her most intimate confidante. Nobody had an inkling of her inner turmoil as she went cheerfully about her duties. On Tuesday when she got home from the surgery her next-door neighbour came in with a bouquet of pink carnations that a local florist had left for her. With a fluttering heart Kate took them into the kitchen, thinking they were from Martin, but the attached card read, 'To thank you for a lovely weekend, from Lisa and Debbie.'

Poor Lisa, she was trying so hard to be friends. Kate wished she could feel the same way towards her, but she couldn't. She believed rightly or wrongly that Simon had been snared into a marriage of convenience.

Then it was Wednesday, her half-day and her date with Angus. He had phoned to say he would pick her up soon after two o'clock as he wanted to make a personal visit before going on to show her the sights of York.

Kate got back to 9, Riverside Terrace just before one, which gave her time for a quick snack before Angus called. It didn't take long to decide what to wear: something casual and ordinary so as not to show Angus up in any way. She had no wish to put him to shame, not that she could imagine Angus feeling ashamed about anything—certainly not how he looked.

She finally settled on a velour leisure-suit, which though by no means shabby had seen better days. She had just finished brushing her hair so that it gleamed like old copper when there came a loud and extended ring at the door which sent Pesky into a frenzy of barking. He thought it was the postman.

'Trust that man to sound like a fire alarm!' Kate muttered under her breath as she hurried downstairs. She opened the door—then stood mute. It had to be Angus, no one else she knew had such unusual-coloured eyes, but in all other aspects he was unrecognisable.

He was wearing an immaculate light-grey suit and with it a darker grey shirt, and the crowning touch—a lavender-hued bow-tie! Somehow he had even managed to tame his hair and it fell across his forehead in a natural wave. It came home to Kate with some force what Rachel had meant by saying that Angus could be a snappy dresser when he liked. Now it was Kate who became acutely aware of her own shortcomings. She looked helplessly down at her suit, then bolted up the stairs, calling over her shoulder that she wouldn't be a minute, she hadn't changed yet.

She came down much more sedately than she went up, now attired in the cream silk dress she had last worn at Martin's wedding, and apologised for not being ready on time. But Angus wasn't deceived. His dark blue eyes twinkled with amusement, he knew very well why she had dashed off to change at the last minute. Oh yes, he knew.

Covering the ground of the vast Vale of York was a new experience for Kate. She sat silent and absorbed as the powerful car swallowed up the miles and Angus pointed out famous landmarks. He told her they were travelling through countryside that was a natural passageway between the Yorkshire Dales and the North York Moors. Two thousand years before it had been the gateway to the North for the advancing Romans.

Kate was more familiar with the cobbled market towns like Yelverthorpe and the smaller villages of the high moors. Here was a different landscape of wide skies and lush pastures and peaceful villages of stone houses surrounded by trees. Trees were more evident here than in the high country. In one village they passed through, sheep wandered about like pet dogs. They grazed on the greensward that edged the river and lumbered about the narrow village street ignoring traffic and pedestrians alike. Some even lay stretched on the steps of the cottages soaking in the sun—no garden was sacrosanct.

'Doesn't anybody protest? Do the villagers mind their gardens being trampled over? asked Kate, amazed.

'Nothing they can do about it,' Angus answered, grinning. 'As long as I can remember sheep have always used this particular village as their private property, and they help bring in the tourists. We'll pass a car park up here and you'll see it's chock-a-block with cars and coaches. The souvenir and craft shops do a roaring trade. Sheep are good for business.

'And then I suppose they have to be eaten!' Kate couldn't resist retorting.

He turned and gave her a quizzical look, his eyebrows lifting sardonically. 'What do you think goes into tins of dog food besides kangaroo? Worn-out old ewes too tough for human consumption? I've often wondered. You think about it too next time you open a tin for Pesky.'

That silenced her and kept her occupied with worrying thoughts long after they had left the attractive village with its sheep and souvenir-hunters behind them.

'And still on the subject,' Angus went on as they accelerated into the fast lane of the major road, 'were you born a vegetarian or did you become one by choice, and if you did—why?'

'Must you always know people's motives?'

'No. Only people who interest me. Come on, Kate, don't be coy, tell me why you won't eat meat?'

Reluctance made her say grudgingly, 'Promise you won't laugh.'

'As if I would!' But his voice was shaking with laughter already.

'About six years ago, just after I'd taken my second MB, I had three unpleasant experiences one after the other. First I saw a documentary on TV about factory farming which churned my stomach. Then I had a meat pie for my lunch which was just going off and that churned my stomach even more, and finally I saw an old film called *Prime Cut* in which someone was murdered and then put through a sausage-making machine. That clinched it! I've been a vegetarian ever since.'

Angus threw back his head and let out such a bellow of laughter it echoed round the car. Kate turned on him. 'Traitor—you promised not to laugh!'

He brushed the back of his hand across his eyes. 'I'm sorry, but I couldn't bottle that up. Oh, you're priceless! I saw that film too, I thought it was jolly good, and as far as I remember it was only the chap's shoes that went through the sausage-machine.'

'That was bad enough, and in any case it was left to us to imagine the rest.' Kate put a hand up to her mouth. 'Do you mind if we talk about something else, I'm beginning to feel a bit queasy.'

Angus stopped laughing, and his hand closed over hers, giving her an understanding squeeze. His hand was cool to the touch. The last time she had felt it closeness it was burning with fever. Diffidently she drew her own hand away, not because she disliked his touch—more the reverse. She had yet to ask herself why he had such an effect on her. It was enough that he did, and she didn't intend to encourage him.

They were approaching the outskirts of York when Angus said, 'You don't mind coming along with me to call on this old fellow I used to know in Yelverthorpe? He lives on his own since his wife died and I never come to York without looking him up. He's in his eighties and has a dicky heart—and well, I wouldn't like to miss a visit. Just in case, you know—'

Kate did. This was a side of Angus she warmed to—going out of his way to keep an eye on a lonely old man.

Mr Wellbrook lived in a small terraced house in a partly demolished street. As they headed in that direction Angus gave Kate a short history of his life which, in the past few years, had had a touch of a Greek tragedy about it.

Mr and Mrs Wellbrook had been gardener and housekeeper to a wealthy landowner in Yelverthorpe, living in a cottage on the estate. They had one son, born late in life, who turned out to be a brilliant scholar and had won a scholarship to a public school. The Wellbrooks had to make great sacrifices to keep him there, as though they had no fees to pay there were other expenses— clothes and books and allowances, etc. But no sacrifice was too much for Jude.

'If Jude is a shortened version of Judas, he was aptly named,' said Angus grimly. 'But he did well, and that was all the payment they wanted. He got a first-class degree and then his Ph.D., and then he got married to a girl he met at college. Not a student, she was doing some holiday job in the kitchen. She had no relatives as far as I knew, I expect she was an orphan.

'The Wellbrooks spent their last penny on that wedding, both Alice and I were invited. You could feel their pride in their son like something tangible, and as for the girl—well, they treated her like the daughter they'd always longed for. I'll cut the rest of this story short, it won't make for happy listening. While the old couple were of use to the young Wellbrooks, like having them to stay at their cottage for holidays or Christmases, and later on looking after the grandchildren while the young pair went off on their own somewhere, they saw quite a lot of their son and daughter-in-law and the grandchildren whom they idolised. Then old man Wellbrook had his first heart attack and the daughter-in-law must have seen the writing on the wall. She didn't want to be lumbered with an invalid father-in-law— besides, by this time Jude was doing very well for himself and the old couple were becoming a liability rather than an asset.

'The wife was the dominating partner of that marriage. Jude always was morally weak, and he was like putty in her hands. It was she who contrived the move to London. Then gradually their letters and phone calls became more and more infrequent and visits up to Yorkshire to see the old folk petered out.

'It's true there wasn't much room in the cottage now that the children were growing bigger, but there was nothing to stop the young Wellbrooks inviting the old couple to stay with them. They had plenty of room in a spacious house in a very nice position near Hampstead Heath. But no such invitation materialised. I think the old people were now an embarrassment to them. The young Wellbrooks were social climbers, and they didn't want their smart new friends to learn about their humble origins.'

Angus slowed down, changed gear and turned into a network of mean streets.

'I shall never forgot the day I was sitting in Mrs Wellbrook's kitchen when the postman called,' he said savagely. 'He handed her a letter returned by the Post Office. To the day I die I shall remember the look on her face as she opened it. It was her last letter to her son asking why they hadn't heard from him. The Post Office had returned it because the addressee had moved and had left no forwarding address.'

Angus's voice took on a steely note. 'I couldn't sit there and watch Mrs Wellbrook's suffering without doing something to help. She wasn't only a patient, she was a good friend. I went off to London to make some enquiries, but Jude Wellbrook had covered his tracks well. All I discovered was that he had emigrated to Canada with his family. I didn't bother to make further equiries then—he obviously didn't want to be traced.'

'Do you mean to say he just cleared out of the country without a word to his mother and father? What kind of a man *is* he!'

Angus gave a deep sigh. 'You tell me,' he said.

They had turned into a street of small run-down houses, and Angus drew up in front of one where a bottle of milk still stood on the doorstep.

'The Wellbrooks moved from a cottage in Yelverthorpe for *this* ?' cried Kate, askance.

'Their employer died and the estate was sold, their cottage with it. They would have been homeless if someone hadn't let them this house at a nominal rent. It's due for demolition, anyway. By this time they didn't care where or how they lived. Mrs Wellbrook died soon after they moved to York— from cardiac failure, according to her death-certificate. From a broken heart, according to Alice, and I can't say I don't agree with her.'

Angus cut the engine and turned round in his seat to face Kate. He saw she was near to tears, and the expression on his rugged face softened. Telling the story had made him angry, seeing how it affected Kate made him regret he had caused her sorrow on this day when he had wanted only to give her pleasure.

'It seems incredible to me that a son could walk out on his parents just like that—without a reason. Why? Because they were old—sick—useless?' Kate asked in bewilderment.

'Or because Jude was brainwashed by his wife? Perhaps she gave an ultimatum—me or them, sort of thing. Don't forget she was without a family herself so had no sense of family ties—perhaps she resented the relationship, perhaps she wanted Jude and the children all to herself, I don't know.' Angus gave a shrug. 'Women are far more unscrupulous than men when it comes to getting their own way. It's no holds barred then.'

Kate had a retort ready for that remark, she was always quick to come to the defence of her own sex. Then she thought of Sandra—and to a lesser degree, Lisa. They had known how to manipulate events for their own benefit.

She gave a defiant toss of her head. 'I don't intend to argue about that,' she said loftily. 'All I know is, I haven't got such power.'

A faint smiled hovered about his mouth as he looked steadily into her eyes. 'Haven't you, Kate?' he said softly. 'I wouldn't say that—not looking at you from the angle of a man susceptible to almond-shaped eyes the colour of sea-mist.'

She quickly lowered her head, conscious of her heightened colour and not wanting to see the teasing glitter that was about to illuminate his dark eyes. She knew he *was* teasing, of course. Men such as Angus McGill didn't resort to honeyed words—they used the direct approach. And in any case, after the unhappy story he had just told her wasn't it insensitive of him to switch so quickly to a romantic mood?

Old Mr Wellbrook was delighted to see Angus, and when Kate was introduced he took her hand gently between his own misshapen hands. He was a gaunt giant of a man with a long thin face, and sloping shoulders. Years of working out of doors in all weathers had twisted his limbs with rheumatism.

But there were no signs of querulousness about his manner—there was no sense of self-pity. He insisted on getting tea for them and brought out a shop cake, apologising because it wasn't up to the standard of the cakes his Ada used to bake.

Kate had the feeling that he was consumed by some inner excitement. His faded eyes had a feverish glitter about them and once or twice he seemed on the point of blurting out something, but he gave them a chance to drink their tea before suddenly leaning forward and tapping Angus on the knee.

'Jude's back!' he said excitedly. 'I seen him—two or three times.'

Angus and Kate exchanged glances. 'He's been to see you?' asked Angus.

'No, he hasna called—he just 'angs around keeping an eye on me. I see him when I got my pension at top o' road. I see him once outside Marks and Spencers in Parliament Street. He don't want me to see him, though—not yet, anyroad. He'd always vanished when I look agen.'

Angus and Kate exchanged another glance, the same thought in both their minds. Mr Wellbrook was in his eighties and his sight was poor—was he seeing what he wanted to see? Kate blinked away ready tears as she looked about the tiny room. There were photographs of his son in every nook and cranny, ranging from babyhood through to schooldays, to a student in his graduation gown, right on to wedding photos, and later with his wife and children.

He had been a fair-haired handsome child and a good-looking young student, but the mature man had a grim expression. Not once in the later photographs was he smiling.

'How long is it since Jude went to Canada?' Angus asked.

'Six—seven years.' Mr Wellbrook leant forward again in the same eager way as if to stress his conviction. 'I know what ye're thinking, tha' I'm kidding meself it's Jude—that mebbe I'm imagining him. But I tell ye, there's nowt wrong up here,' and he tapped his forehead. 'I see my Jude—I'll stake my life on 't. An' I know my Jude. He feels sheepish like after all this time—he's feeling his way like till he can pluck up courage to knock on t'door. But he's come back, my lad—he's come back to me. That shows he still cares—that he's watching over me like.'

Kate collected up the used tea-things and took them out to the kitchen to deal with, leaving the two men on their own. She felt she could no longer listen—it was all so pitiful.

Later, on their way to the city centre, she asked Angus what he thought about it. Was it possible that Jude Wellbrook could have returned to England and was secretly watching over his father?

Angus gave a sceptical growl. 'Can you imagine Jude Wellbrook coming thousands of miles just to play hide and seek? For what reason anyway? If he wants to see his father why not call on him openly?'

'Perhaps as Mr Wellbrook said, he's too ashamed. Perhaps he just wants to assure himself that his father's all right.'

Angus shook his head. 'You're just as bad as the old man—indulging in fantasy. I think poor old Wellbrook is suffering from hallucinations, it's not uncommon at his age. He longs to see his boy again—I imagine he thinks of little else these days—and if he believes he sees him that's nearly as good as really seeing him. It's given him an interest in life, something he lost when his wife died. He seems more chipper today than he has in weeks.'

By now they had joined a main thoroughfare and Angus drew into a parking space at the kerbside. He looked at his watch.

'We haven't left much time to explore York. I wanted to show you the Minster and the Folk Museum, possibly the Railway Museum and to walk the wall—you'd have a panoramic view of the city from there. But the Minster alone would take up most of the afternoon, it would be criminal to do it in less. We'll have to visit York again just to go over the Minster thoroughly.'

Kate hardly took heed of his words, her thoughts were still on old Mr Wellbrook. In some ways his feelings for his son ran parallel with hers for Simon, and brought home to her how important it was to keep the family united. How tenuous the ties that held mothers and fathers and daughters and sons together—ties that could be broken by a hasty word. She thought of Lisa and her offering of the pink carnations. Could she, Kate, afford to lose Simon because she couldn't accept Lisa? She knew she couldn't.

'I'd like to do some shopping,' she said, making up her mind suddenly. 'I want to buy a belated wedding present.'

Angus thought there was something rather appealing about her at that moment—something in her expression that showed uncertainty and a certain fear. Her eyes looked bright green in the afternoon light, and the wind had blown her hair into a tangle of curls, tiny red-gold tendrils fluttering against her cheeks. Gone for the present was the illusion of a clever and self-confident doctor. Angus saw only a young girl vulnerable to fortune. He wanted to take her hand in his, to offer comfort, but remembering how he had been rebuffed before, refrained. He could wait, and Kate was worth waiting for.

'I can leave the car here,' he said. 'We're within walking distance of the shops, and I'll take you to Stonegate. Nobody visits York without seeing Stonegate, and we can take in part of the wall on the way.'

During that walk Kate fell in love with York. She was seeing it at its best in the summer sunshine. Angus was right. No one could do justice to York in one short afternoon—not even in a day, or a week.

Meanwhile Kate looked in all the jewellers they passed, looking for a likely wedding present, then decided on one whose prices were more in line with her pocket. She had seen what she wanted now, a small round glass paperweight with a beautiful sculptured butterfly trapped in its heart.

It was too small to be of any use as a real paperweight. It was an object of beauty only, something to be treasured, to be admired. Kate knew it would be more sensible to buy something practical like sheets or towels—but this was more than a present, it was peace-offering, and she hoped Lisa would see it as that.

'That's a very generous gift,' Angus remarked when they were outside once more.

'Not so much generous as overdue,' she said, and laughed somewhat tremulously.

The bright sunlight in the street was dazzling. Kate was in the act of putting on her sunglasses when she saw opposite the familiar name of a Bond Street store. 'Have I got time to do some more shopping?' she asked hopefully.

'You certainly have not! The shops will be closing soon—and I'm hungry. Aren't you?'

She admitted she was.

'Good. Do you like Indian? We'll be able to indulge in our own tastes there.'

Oh yes, she liked Indian food. After all, she pointed out to him, many orthodox Hindus were strict vegetarians.

Twilight was settling over the Dales as much later they drove towards Yelverthorpe after one of the happiest days Kate had known for a long time. The visit to the old gardener had somehow banished the feeling of constraint between herself and Angus— constraint only on her part, realised Kate. Angus was an entertaining companion with a fund of stories to relate, and told in that fruity voice of his she could have listened to for hours.

The meal in the Indian restaurant had been delightful and they lingered over it, sipping a light sparkling wine that rapidly loosened Kate's tongue and she found herself talking freely about her student days and her life with her brother before she came North. But she was sufficiently in control of herself to avoid mentioning Martin, though it took some doing as he was so much a part of her early life. Once or twice she nearly blurted out his name and only just stopped herself in time. But Angus wasn't fooled. She could tell by the penetrating looks he kept giving her that he had guessed the unmentioned name.

After the meal they had wandered for more than a hour around the ancient streets of York, finally walking down to the river and having a last drink on a moored pleasure boat that had been converted into a pub. There was the sound of piano music coming from the saloon, but they sat out on deck to drink their brandy, watching the waters of the Ouse turning black as daylight faded from the sky.

Neither had much to say on the return journey. Angus was in a thoughtful mood, and Kate had to struggle against sleep. She had put in a busy morning at the practice, they had walked for miles over stone slabs and cobbles—she in a flimsy pair of shoes—now fresh air and drink combined were taking their toll.

'Give in—put your head on my shoulder,' invited Angus once, but she declined. Not because she didn't trust him—in her present mood she didn't trust herself.

Then it was all spoilt. The pleasant day, the happy camaraderie, her appreciation of his kindness—all wiped out in a few moments. Angus drew up outside her little house, she thanked him, and was about to invite him in for coffee, when he turned her round to face him and said softly, 'Kiss me, Kate.'

Why not? Where was the harm in a kiss—a small return for what he had done for her? She leant forward to bestow a light friendly kiss on his cheek—but that wasn't what Angus intended. She found herself imprisoned in his powerful arms; she felt his lips warm and eager and demanding on hers, and suddenly she found herself responding with an ardour that disturbed and excited her at the same time. Then she tried to draw away, realising that Angus wasn't going to stop at kissing.

She struggled to free herself from his grip and he laughed low in his throat.

'What is it, Kate—are you frightened to be yourself? Don't worry, my sweet, I won't do anything against your wishes.'

'Then let go of me—'

'You don't want me to let go, I can feel you trembling. You're trembling because you can't control your feelings. Haven't you ever been roused like this before? Oh, Kate, sweet Kate, be honest— I do mean something to you, don't I?'

It was true—but she would bite her tongue out before admitting it! And for him to guess it—no, not guess—to *know*, that was what she couldn't face. This wasn't love, not this sudden rush of passion—this wasn't what she had felt for Martin. All her recent dislike of Angus came flooding back. He was so sure of himself—so sure of *her* —that was the most shaming part. She struggled more than ever, pushing against him, and suddenly he released her.

In the half-light his eyes glinted menacingly. 'What's stopped you?' he demanded roughly. 'Thoughts of your precious Martin?'

'No, it's not Martin,' she cried passionately. 'I don't like being taken for granted—it's too humiliating, that's why!' Her heart was pounding in her ears, she was breathing heavily and she could have wept for having her lovely day end in this unseemly brawling match. She climbed out of the car and slammed the door after her. Angus leant forward and caught hold of her wrist.

'Do you mean to tell me that if it had been Martin who kissed you as I did just now, you wouldn't have given in to him?'

But Martin had never kissed her like that—he had never aroused feelings that had sent her to the edge of an ecstasy so fierce she had drawn back in alarm.

She shut her eyes, trying to conjure up an image of Martin, trying to use his memory as a shield against this man who had such power over her—but the image when it came was of Angus. Angus with his lively dark blue eyes and wolfish grin.

Angus mistook the reason for her silence.

'You still love Martin, don't you?' His voice was scathing. 'And *you* talk glibly about humiliation! Don't you find it humiliating to hanker afer a man who's thrown you over for another woman? Who doesn't care a fig for you!'

There was no excuse for what Kate said next, because she chose her words carefully. But she also lost her temper, and the words she uttered so deliberately were born from a rush of wounded pride.

'If Martin doesn't love me, why did he go to the trouble of phoning me from Alicante?' she cried out with emotion. 'Yes, that's made you sit up, hasn't it! He phoned me on Sunday evening. He said he just wanted to hear my voice because he missed me so. He may have married another woman, but he still loves me—me, do you hear?— *me* —!'

She stopped in mid-sentence, arrested by the look that raked her like a scourge. When Angus spoke his voice was icy with contempt.

'In that case I'll leave you to your dreams and your shoddy little triumph,' he said, and with engine revving he roard off into the gathering darkness.

CHAPTER SEVEN

KATE ran blindly into the house and slammed the front door behind her. The first thing that came to hand when she entered the kitchen was the teapot, and she picked it up and hurled it at the wall. Her action released in her an anguished fury, but it didn't do the teapot any good. With a yelp of fear Pesky bolted into the front room and hid under the sofa. Kate followed him, flinging herself down on the same sofa and bursting into tears. Pesky struggled out of his hiding-place backwards, fled back to the kitchen and jumped into his basket where he waited, trembling.

Presently, Kate joined him. She had recovered from her storm of weeping, and was ashamed of herself for losing control. She went on her hands and knees and began to pick up the pieces of broken china, and on the last piece she cut herself.

Her tears began to flow again, this time with rage and frustration. 'Damn and blast it!' she yelled at the top of her voice. She held her finger under the cold water tap. "Damn and blast the teapot. Damn and blast all men. Damn and blast Martin and Simon and—and that prig Angus!' She heard Pesky whimpering and glared down at him. 'And damn and blast you too, you—you yapping scrubbing-brush!'

Weakly, she leant against the sink for support.

She couldn't shut out from her mind the look in Angus's eyes when he had hurled those final wounding words at her. How dared he say such things—how dared he even think such things!

Pesky whimpered again, and Kate dried her finger and went across to him. Poor little pet, what had he done to deserve this? He was slobbering from anxiety and yet at the same time he was wagging his tail. She picked him up and buried her face in his fur.

Carrying him, she returned to the front room and sat with him on her lap, talking to him as if he were a confidante—which for the time being, he was.

'I shouldn't have shouted at you Pesky,' she murmured, fondling his ear. 'I couldn't help myself, something just went inside me. Oh, Pesky, darling Pesky—what a rotten miserable thing it is to be in love! It's not happiness or roses all the way—it's misery and doubt and heartache, and it kills—it kills with pain.' She began to sob again, dry-eyed and with her throat aching. 'I love him, Pesky. I realise now I love him, and yet how is it possible to be in love with someone you loathe? He's a bully and he's arrogant and he's—he's *insufferable* and he despises me, he made that plain enough, but I love him. It explains so much that didn't make sense before—the effect he always has on me and the feeling of power that excites me. I never felt this way about Martin. Poor Martin—I never loved him enough to hate him. He wasn't capable of causing such strong emotions in me!'

Long after midnight, when sleep still eluded her, she kept asking herself over and over again—how could she have believed all these years that her love for Martin was the real thing? How had she been able to deceive herself, and for that matter, Martin too? She *had* loved him—loved him in the way she loved Simon, and hadn't realised the difference until Angus came along and aroused her from her complacent belief that love was just another sort of comfort. He had stirred in her feelings she did not know she possessed, had awakened strong sensations of desire. But did that matter now? She could never risk letting him discover the true state of her feelings towards him, not after the look he had given her before he drove away. She could take anything from him but contempt.

The Town Hall clock struck three and she counted the strokes with a sense of finality. So what had she achieved by exchanging one unrequited love for another? Only the bitter knowledge that she would have got over Martin, but it would not be so easy to forget Angus. The effect he had on her was more far-reaching, his grip on her emotions more tenacious.

The following day she turned up at the practice with eyes hollow from lack of sleep, but she got through a busy work load with such determination that though many anxious glances were directed at her during the morning, nothing was said.

Dr Lambert kept his opinion to himself until Kate had gone off on her rounds. Then, 'That girl's burning the candle at both ends,' he said emphatically to Audrey. 'Did you notice how washed-out she looked? Out dancing all night, I shouldn't wonder. Oh, what it is to be young!'

But Kate didn't feel all that young as she crossed the bridge to Yelverthorpe over the water, she felt as old as time. Does one ever grow out of yearning—of aching for the sight of a loved one? she wondered.

Sunday was another day spent on her own. Rachel and Benjy were off to Whitby, and though she had been asked to join them Kate had made the excuse that she had to catch up on some housework. But that wasn't the real reason. She knew Rachel was astute enough to tell when anything was wrong. Kate couldn't risk it—not yet. The knowledge that she loved Angus was so new and so precious to her that she didn't want to share it with anybody else for the present.

Lunchtime came and went; Pesky was getting restless without his daily walk and Kate roused herself out of her lethargy. She fetched Pesky's lead, changed into walking shoes, got her jacket from upstairs and off they went.

There was a small park to the north of the town. The walk there and back with a rest in between was about Pesky's limit. Today was perfect for walking, not too hot, with great billowing clouds scudding before a south-westerly breeze. The park was full of Sunday strollers, dog-walkers and children—the latter in a corner fenced off as a play area. Dogs weren't allowed there, or off their leads anywhere in the park.

Kate was fortunate enough to find an unoccupied bench and Pesky flopped down at her feet, his tongue lolling out of his mouth as he panted. Suddenly all tiredness fell from him and he sprang to his feet and began to bark in a frenzy of excitement. He had seen a friend, a large Clumber spaniel approaching—Shandy!

Kate's heart flipped, then began to thump unsteadily but it wasn't Angus out walking the dog, it was his sister Alice. She recognised Kate at once and came hurrying up, her broad face alight with pleasure.

'May I share your seat, my dear, I'm feeling a wee bit weary. This animal has dragged me all the way from the market place - he doesn't feel his walk is complete unless we do a circuit of the park. And how are you? If you don't mind me saying so, you're looking just a mite peaky. Been overworking, I suspect.'

Alice sat down beside her and tightened her hold on Shandy's leash. The two dogs went into the ritual of circling, then sniffing at each other before settling down side by side. Alice smiled at them fondly, then turned the same smile on Kate.

'Well, well, and isn't this bonny meeting like this? I've been looking forward to seeing you again. I feel I didn't really show how grateful I was the day Angus had his attack of malaria. But I've been hearing all about you from him. He told me about meeting you out with Pesky and the two of you going to York. I hope he thanked you properly for being so kind to him the day of the wedding. My brother's manners are not all that they should be, I'm afraid.'

'He got over his bout of malaria very quickly,' Kate put in hastily.

'Oh aye, the man's as strong as a horse. What's more he hasn't had an attack since. But the dear Lord knows what's the matter with him these past three days. I can't do anything to please him. He's worse than a bear with a sore head, though I never know what that means really—I've never seen a bear with a sore head.' Alice shaded her eyes with her hand as she looked about her. 'Isn't it pleasant here, my dear,' she went on musingly. 'Just smell that heliotrope, the sun has drawn out the perfume. It's so evocative—it reminds me of Jersey. Have you ever been to Jersey?'

Kate was relieved to find she wasn't expected to answer, or even to contribute anything to the conversation. Alice was content with a yes or a no in the right places, she just wanted somebody to talk to. Mostly she talked about her brother; her life revolved around him.

She jumped from one subject to the other, but she took Kate by surprise when she suddenly asked, 'Did you hear about the poor landlord of the Drover's Arms?'

'Do you mean Bob Lewis?' Kate remembered the name without difficulty. She often thought back on that stolen visit to the moorland inn.

'Aye, that's the one. Weel now, Angus told me about taking you to the inn for a wee bite, and how he thought the landlord was looking unwell, and how he intended to go back and see him again. Weel, the other night Angus was so restless he didn't know what to do with himself, then he remembered the poor landlord and away he went. I don't mind telling you I was glad to see the back of him, he was driving me to distraction with his pacing up and down. And it's as well he decided to go and see this Mr Lewis—he found him in a very poor way, on the point of collapse, in fact. Angus arranged for an ambulance to get him to hospital at once and the poor man was operated on as soon as they reached hospital—not a mite too soon, Mr Maude said. Mr Maude is the senior surgeon—but och, you know that already, don't you?'

'How is Mr Lewis now?' asked Kate.

'Coming along nicely, dear, but of course it's early days as yet. He had an extremely large duodenal ulcer—he was taken to hospital just in time, according to Mr Maude. The ulcer was in danger of perforating. If Angus hadn't decided to go off to the inn that particular night goodness knows what would have happened to the poor man.'

'What night was that?' asked Kate, but she had already guessed.

'Wednesday. Wasn't that the day you both went to York?'

Kate nodded dumbly, thinking to herself that the only one to have got any benefit from that particular day was the unfortunate Bob Lewis.

Alice went on relentlessly, 'Angus was in such a funny mood that night, I often feel ashamed now to think how impatient I got with him. If it weren't for Angus poor Mr Lewis—weel, we won't dwell on that.' Alice gave a reflective sigh. 'I often think Angus would have made an excellent general surgeon himself. Have you noticed his hands—a surgeon's hands, I always think, strong and reliable— Why, my dear, you're not thinking of going, are you?' for Kate had suddenly got to her feet.

'I'm afraid I must. I've left jobs undone at home.'

'I've driven you away with my blethering. And going on like I do about my brother! But I can't help it—I'm such a proud sister.'

'I enjoyed hearing about your brother.' And Kate had up to a point, then it had become unbearable with its sweet torment.

Alice had also risen, but reluctantly—she had enjoyed her chat with Kate. It was not often that young ones had the patience to listen to the maunderings of middle-aged women, but Kate had, and with interest, though Alice had sometimes noticed shadows of distress flicker across her face as if something was worrying her.

'Weel, I suppose I must take Shandy for his wee constitutional around the park,' she said now, smiling at the two dogs who were showing eagerness to get moving. 'It's a pleasure to watch the two doggies,' she observed to Kate. 'They get on so well together. But then we all do don't we? You and I, and Angus and you. I bless the day that other young couple got married—it brought you two together. There, I've made you blush, but you mustn't mind me, my dear. I always say what I think. And I've been waiting for a nice young girl like you to come along and knock some of the rough edges off that brother of mine!'

Kate parted from Alice at the entrance to the park, glad to make her escape. She had found the other woman's frankness disconcerting, and fervently hoped that she didn't talk to Angus in the same vein. Kate told herself wryly that she had no wish to smooth away Angus's rough edges. She loved him in spite of his rough edges. No—*because* of them. It had been a relief to learn that he was shortly off to Scotland. It would be just as well if they did not see one another for several weeks, then it would not be so embarrassing when they came face to face once more.

Kate had just finished a busy morning in the gynaecology operating theatre. The last patient, a woman of forty with a history of fibroids, had had a hysterectomy. When Kate had called on her the previous day to give her a general check-up, she had found her in tears.

'I'm sorry, Doctor, for being so weepy,' she said apologetically. 'But I've been lying here thinking. I won't be a complete woman any more—I won't be able to have any more children.'

'At your age, Mrs Lloyd, were you planning to increase your family?'

'Of course not, that's where I'm being so silly. I've got three lovely kids already. But it's just— well, lying here brooding, I think all sorts of things.

For instance, I heard somewhere once that after a woman has her womb removed she turns into a crank or gets fat.'

Oh dear, thought Kate, wherever do patients get hold of these far–fetched ideas? 'I can reassure you, Mrs Lloyd,' she said, 'that you will *not* turn into a crank, but you'll certainly become a much healthier woman. A lot of women have said they felt ten years younger after having a hysterectomy. You're suffering from operation nerves—you'll feel better after your premedication. And as for putting on weight—well, that's just a question of eating the right food.'

Kate had left Mrs Lloyd in a much happier state of mind than when she found her. Now the operation was successfully completed, the patient was in the recovery room, and Kate was free until two-thirty when she was due back at the practice.

A post-luncheon hush had fallen over most of the wards. The occupants were either asleep or lying expectantly with eyes on the clock. The doors would be open to visitors any moment now. Kate decided to take the opportunity to go along to see how Bob Lewis was getting on. She knew he was in Fletcher Ward, one of the men's surgicals.

She found him in a bay of six beds, two of them unoccupied. The other three patients were too engrossed with their visitors to take notice of Kate; She was just another figure in a white coat.

Bob Lewis was sleeping. He still looked a very sick man, but Kate fancied the fretful lines around his mouth and eyes were not so noticeable now. His chart and notes showed that he was making slow but steady progress.

But Kate thought how sad his locker looked—it

was bare but for a jug of water. There were no get-well cards, no flowers, no sweets or fruit, unlike those of his companions whose locker tops were crowded with offerings from well-wishers. Perhaps Bob Lewis had no relatives near enough to visit—and it was quite probable he had no friends either. His behaviour in the Drover's Arms bore out that idea. The empty locker seemed to Kate like a symbol of an empty life, and she felt she must do something about it. Mr Lewis might not thank her—he might even snub her, but she would risk that.

She hurried down to the shop on the ground floor and returned with apples and oranges and a box of fruit pastilles. There was a plastic bowl inside the locker, and she had just finished filling it with the fruit when she became aware that Bob Lewis was awake and watching her.

He didn't recognise her, of course, but Kate thought there was a flicker of a smile in his eyes before the lids came down again. He was still drowsy.

There was no point in staying any longer. She was very much on edge in case Angus made a sudden appearance. But she was safely out of the hospital and on the way to the car park before she spotted him coming from the direction of the dental block. She held her breath, dreading in case he looked in her direction, but he kept his gaze fixed straight ahead, walking briskly towards the hospital.

At the sight of his burly, unkempt figure all the love she felt for him and which she had hoped she had suppressed came flooding back. She watched him until he was out of sight, tormenting herself with a useless longing. What was to prevent her running after him and letting him see how she felt?

Nothing but the conviction that he would be more amused than flattered.

August came in with lowered skies and sudden outbursts of chilling rain. Then the sun would reappear and the pavements steam until the next lot of black clouds blew in from the west. Kate received an ecstatic letter from Lisa thanking her for the paperweight. She wrote that she had never seen anything so beautiful in her life before; she suggested that Kate should come and stay with them whenever she had any free time—that was if she didn't mind sharing a room with Debbie.

Kate smiled wryly over that, thinking Miss Debbie might have something to say on the matter. Actually Kate had not yet made any arrangements about a holiday, though she had two weeks due to her in September. She had toyed with the idea of staying with her old college friend Carole Bircham in London, so that she could catch up on the latest shows and do a round of the stores, but Carole had now moved to Sussex, working as a school medical officer, so that idea was scotched.

Kate had seen nothing of Angus since that glimpse in the hospital car park, and she sometimes wondered if he had already left for Scotland, then out of the blue one day there was a phone call from him at the surgery. It was just before six o'clock, and she was about to start her evening clinic. At the sound of his voice Kate's heart began to pound uncomfortably, and she felt her hand tighten involuntarily on the phone, but with an effort she managed to hide her agitation. 'Dr Murray speaking,' came out quite normally.

'Ah, Kate, I'm glad I've caught you—I have some sad news, I'm afraid.' His own voice sounded jaded, she thought. 'Old Mr Wellbrook died at midday today.'

Thoughts of York came to Kate's mind, and the memory of the afternoon's joy that had turned to nightfall's stupid misunderstanding.

'Was it his heart?' she asked quietly

'No, it was an accident. He was knocked down by a car and died shortly afterwards. I was with him at the time. I would like to talk to you about it, over a drink perhaps. Any chance this evening?'

Kate hesitated. She couldn't see how they could meet even on neutral ground without considerable embarrassment—yet in a small town like Yelverthorpe she couldn't go on avoiding him, and in any case, she wanted to know what had happened to Mr Wellbrook.

She told Angus she would be finished about eight, and he said he would meet her then. He was waiting outside the practice when she came out. 'Have you got your car here?' he asked.

'Its parked just round the corner—'

'Well, come in mine, I'll bring you back to pick up your car later. It's only to the Black Lion. We could have walked if it weren't for this rain.'

She was sorry he had chosen that particular inn out of the many in Yelverthorpe, it was where Martin used to stay, and her memories of it were not without pain. But it had the reputation of being the best hostelry in the town, it was comfortable and comparatively quiet and there were real, not ceramic, logs burning in the grate. Also they found a corner that gave them complete privacy.

Angus ordered a Cinzano and lemonade for Kate and a pint of bitter for himself. His manner was quite affable and so far he had made no mention of their last encounter. Perhaps in the circumstances he thought it best not to allude to it, even pretend it had never happened.

'How did you know about Mr Wellbrook?' asked Kate.

'The police phoned me—they'd found my name and address when going through the old man's wallet. I set off for York as soon as I heard.'

'How did the accident happen?'

Angus replaced his glass on the drip mat. The death of Mr Wellbrook had affected him deeply, his sadness was reflected both in his voice and his expression, and his eyes had a strange questioning look as if searching for an answer to a problem.

'You remember the old man told us he was convinced that he had seen his son on several occasions? He told me just before he died that he saw Jude again this morning when he went up to the post office to fetch his pension. He was so adamant that I almost found myself believing him. This time, he said, his son didn't vanish as before— he just stood there on the other side of the road smiling across at him. And that's what did for poor old Wellbrook—that smile. He took it as a sign of reconciliation—he started off across the road straight into the path of a passing car, and—well, that's it.' Angus slumped forward and rested his face in his hands. He looked as if he was feeling the effects of the long drive to York and back and the distressing interlude in between.

'Do you think it *could* have been his son?' Kate said hopefully.

Angus shook his head. 'No, I do not—work it out for yourself. If Jude Wellbrook had been there, standing on the opposite pavement, he would have witnessed the accident. Surely then he would have come to his father's aid? Anyone would do that,

even for a stranger. But where is he? He didn't
turn up at the hospital. No, he was just an image
conjured up out of a sick old man's loneliness—out
of his longing to see his son again.'

Kate's eyes misted over, and she swallowed back
tears. Angus hadn't convinced her. She still believed
that Jude Wellbrook had come over to England
purposely to see his father, but someone or
something had prevented him from making contact.
A promise to his wife?—or his own guilt-ridden
shame? She shrugged such ideas away. What did it
matter now, old Mr Wellbrook was dead and free
from any further hurt.

She came out of her reverie to find Angus
studying her closely. His eyes, though red-rimmed
with weariness, were also alert and watchful.

'Penny for them?' he said. He had thrown off his
melancholy, and there was even a hint of the old
devilment about him. 'It looked from your expression
as if you were murdering someone in your heart.
Do you hate whoever it is that much, Kate?'

It was good to hear her name on his lips again,
good to believe that the ugly incident that had
marred their visit to York was now buried and
forgotten. She managed a fitful smile. 'No, I'm not
a good hater—I've tried, but it doesn't work.' She
had once believed she had hated him. When—a
hundred years ago? 'Actually, I was thinking about
Jude Wellbrook, but I don't hate him; I pity him
rather. But what did Mr Wellbrook tell you about
him? Did he think Jude had changed—looked
older?'

'Kate, don't forget there *was* no Jude, and don't
forget either that poor old Wellbrook was dying
and had difficulty in speaking clearly. All I know is
that he died a happy man because he thought

there'd been a reconciliation with his son. And that, after all, is what really matters.'

A silence fell between them then, but it was not an uncomfortable silence. From time to time Kate glanced surreptitiously across at Angus. He was deep in thought, his forehead furrowed in a frown. Kate wished she had the courage to stretch out her hand to smooth the furrows away. She wanted to see Angus smile again, even to give her one of those wolfish grins that sent a shiver down her spine. He looked up once and their eyes met. Kate went crimson, hoping her expression hadn't given her away. But he didn't appear to notice her confusion, his mind was on other things.

'I've been asked to take charge of the funeral arrangements,' he told her. 'I'm bringing the old man back to Yelverthorpe to be buried, to be with his wife. He did it for her, it's only proper I should do it for him—they're Yelverthorpe folk and belong here in the churchyard. The funeral is next Monday. Will you be able to come?'

Without hesitating she said she would, and asked about flowers.

'Just something simple, Mr Wellbrook didn't like show. It will be a quiet affair.' Angus stirred himself, straightening his shoulders as if they ached. 'Now what about another drink?'

But Kate refused. She could tell Angus had a lot on his mind, Perhaps more details to arrange about the funeral. And his holiday, had that been postponed? He would have plans to make about that too.

He drove her back to where she had left her car, and this time their leave taking was in sharp contrast to that of the previous occasion. They were both so casual with each other, in such good control of their feelings, that they could have passed for chance acquaintances. Yet Kate could not help thinking (and hoping) that when they shook hands Angus held on to hers a little longer than was actually necessary.

She drove back to Riverside Terrace in better heart than she had been in for some time. At least there was goodwill between Angus and herself again. Could that be the foundation on which to build a closer relationship?

CHAPTER EIGHT

Two days later Angus phoned again to give Kate more details about the funeral, and she took the opportunity to ask whether Alice would be there.

'Oh yes, nothing would keep her away, she thought the world of the Wellbrooks. By the way—' Angus paused, then made a sound as if he was clearing his throat, or could it have been a chuckle? 'I called in to see Bob Lewis yesterday. He was much improved, even sitting up. I noticed he'd acquired some fruit and some sweets and asked him if he'd had a visitor. But he said no, that an angel with red hair had brought them. He was quite serious too!' Angus chuckled again, there was no mistaking it for anything else but a chuckle this time. 'It was you, of course—nice going, Kate.'

Kate was glad of the anonymity of the phone, Angus couldn't see the pleasure his words had given her. 'Who's going to take care of Mr Lewis when he's discharged?' she asked, carefully ignoring Angus's last remark.

'I understand his wife's sister has been in touch. She and her husband are willing to come and manage the Drover's Arms for a time, and if all goes well, they'll stay on permanently. Bob Lewis may acquire a housekeeper and a partner if that's the case. Perhaps even get back to his old standard.'

Kate thought of the bareness and cheerlessness of

the bar parlour. 'I wish them luck, but what they really need are customers,' she said.

'They'll get them,' answered Angus with conviction.

It rained heavily on Monday. A weekend of fine weather ended in a thunderstorm late on Sunday night. When Kate drew her curtains that evening she saw that menacing clouds were building high above the horizon and the sky had the threatening, sulphurous effect that usually preceded a storm. It broke just before midnight, while Kate was still reading in bed. She put down her book and turned off the light. A part of her exalted in the untamed fury of the storm. It was as if nature was showing it could still get the upper hand of man. It put some things in their proper perspective.

At least the rain solved the problem of what to wear at the funeral. She had been worried about that as her summery clothes were either too brightly-coloured or unsuitable in other ways. Her raincoat was a charcoal grey colour with a matching hat. She put on low-heeled shoes too as she knew the ground in the churchyard would be a quagmire after the night's deluge.

Dr Barnes surprised her by saying he would take her as he was going too. He had known the Wellbrooks fairly well as their late employer had been an old friend of his. It was Kate's first ride in a Rolls-Royce, and when the engine was started it sounded to her no more than a gentle sigh. They took the hill out of town as quietly and easily as if they were on the level and purred to a stop in Church Lane by the lich-gate.

The path up to the church was lined with wreaths and sheaves of flowers, and Angus was completely wrong in his prediction that it would only be a quiet funeral. The church was packed. The last time Kate

had been to the parish church was the occasion of
Martin's wedding—but she wouldn't let herself dwell
on that now. She thought instead of all these friends
of James Wellbrook who had come to pay their last
respects. She recognised some of her patients, and
others were among the town's shopkeepers and
traders, and there were a few from the big houses
around. But most of those present were like James
Wellbrook himself—poor and humble. Poor!—how
wrong she was to think that. Old Mr Wellbrook had
been anything but poor—he'd been rich in the things
that mattered, like love and respect and friendship.

After the burial the mourners drifted away in twos
and threes, and Alice came up to speak to Kate. Her
eyes were red from weeping and her black-gloved
hands fiddled nervously with a handkerchief. Angus
had stayed behind to have a word with the
gravediggers; now his attention was focused on a man
sheltering in the porch. Kate followed his gaze. The
man was a stranger to her—she was sure he wasn't
from Yelverthorpe. He was tall and lean with hollow
cheeks and thinning hair. His glasses effectively
masked all expression in his eyes. There was no
resemblance to the handsome young man Kate had
seen in the photographs in the small house in York,
but somehow she knew this was Jude Wellbrook. A
quick glance at Angus was sufficient to tell her he
was of the same mind. She had been right, then—and
Angus wrong. She was glad, it showed that Jude
Wellbrook wasn't the inhuman creature they had
thought him. He *had* cared about his father.

'Angus is arranging to have the cut flowers delivered
to local hospitals,' Alice was telling Kate. The two of
them had stopped to read the inscriptions on the
wreaths, Alice waiting for Angus who had now been
buttonholed by Dr Barnes. She sighed on a note of

satisfaction. 'Well, it was a grand send-off for the old man and I'm sure he was up above watching it all. It must give him pleasure to know he was so well remembered. And what are you doing with yourself now, Kate? Can you come back to the house for a wee bite?'

'Thank you, but I've got to get back to the surgery with Dr Barnes.' Kate hesitated, then plunged on, 'Are you still going to Scotland?'

'Yes, my dear—we had to postpone our visit, but we'll be off first thing in the morning. Not a day too soon for Angus, he's looking a mite tired lately—and he's always going into what my mother would have called a brown study. Sometimes I feel I can't get through to him. I'm glad to say he's decided to travel by Motorail—at least he'll be spared the long drive. I have everything packed ready. Och now, here come the men.'

Dr Barnes raised his hat as he greeted Alice. 'Come under my umbrella, Miss McGill, you'll get so wet,' he said with old-fashioned courtesy. They walked ahead exchanging chit-chat, leaving Kate and Angus to follow. Kate looked back; the man she believed to be Jude Wellbrook had left the church porch and was now standing on his own by the unfilled grave with the rain falling relentlessly on his bare head.

Angus watched him for a while in silence, then said gruffly, 'I can almost feel it in my heart to pity that poor bastard, though he had scant pity for his own father. I don't envy him—he looks as if he's in purgatory.'

'So it *is* Jude Wellbrook—it's been Jude Wellbrook all along. Poor Mr Wellbrook was right.' There was no triumph in Kate's voice, just a sadness.

'No, he was not right, Kate. I wish I could say he

was. Jude Wellbrook is only here because I shamed him into coming.'

'I—I don't understand.' Kate stared at Angus. The rain had plastered his hair to his forehead, and was dripping off his nose and his chin and his ears, but he seemed impervious to the discomfort. The usual glitter in his dark blue eyes was missing and a look of weary dejection had taken over instead. 'How did you shame him? Have you been in contact with him?' Kate asked.

'I phoned him in Ontario the day his father died.'

'But—but I thought you said you didn't know his address.'

'I didn't at the time he emigrated, but I made it my business to find it out when his mother died. I wrote to him then, but he ignored my letter, so this time I phoned. I told him about his father's death and the manner of his dying, and I gave him the exact time of the funeral, and I also gave him the times of flights to Heathrow and Leeds. I made it impossible for him to refuse me.'

Kate could well imagine that. Angus's mouth was like a steel trap closed against rejection. 'How did Jude take the news of his father's death?' she asked.

'Like a cold fish—monosyllabic, lacking in all feeling. But that brushed off me, I didn't care how he felt as long as he turned up for the funeral.'

Kate turned to take another look at the motionless figure at the graveside. 'So you were right after all,' she said pensively. 'Mr Wellbrook *had* conjured up his son out of his longing to see him again. It's ironic really when you come to think about it. Just an illusion, but it helped Mr Wellbrook to die a happy man.'

'Life is full of ironies. Sometimes I think of fate as a kind of malignant witch looking down on us mortals from a distance—screwing up our lives and having a good laugh as we try to entangle ourselves from her clutches.'

Kate was startled by this sudden outburst of bitterness. The deep full voice resounded with an inner despair.

'I didn't realise this episode with the Wellbrooks had affected you so deeply,' she said, visibly shaken.

'I wasn't thinking of the Wellbrooks,' Angus answered bleakly. Abruptly he took her arm. 'Come along—let's get out of this bloody rain.'

A week later Simon and Lisa and Debbie came to Yelverthorpe for a few days' holiday. Simon had invested in a small car since their last visit and they could now afford to stay at a hotel instead of imposing on Kate, but they did ask if she minded putting Debbie up.

They said she was nervous of sleeping by herself in a strange hotel, but Kate thought it more likely that Simon and Lisa were looking forward to a few evenings on their own. After all, they had had no honeymoon.

Lisa had made a great many changes to her appearance. Either she now had more money to spend on herself or Simon had taken her in hand. She had had her hair cut by an expert and gold highlights put in, and her dress was in the latest style and fitted perfectly. She still used no make-up but had had her eyelashes dyed, and this was a great improvement, lending to her eyes a much-needed lustre. But Debbie hadn't changed much. She still stared out at the world with hostile unchildlike eyes, and Kate noticed that she still assiduously avoided any contact with Simon.

On the Sunday Simon and Lisa went off for the

day, leaving Debbie with Kate. Debbie sat martyr-
like all morning in the front room, refusing every
overture of friendship on Kate's part.

'Would you like a glass of orange squash? A
biscuit, then? A piece of chocolate? Right!' Kate
suddenly lost patience. 'Would you like a good
shaking instead?' she said, half joking, half meaning
it.

Debbie's reaction shattered her. The child jumped
down from her chair and backed against the wall,
staring at Kate with wide fearful eyes, making Kate
feel like some kind of monster. She hurried across to
Debbie and tried to cuddle her, but Debbie strained
away from her with her back arched.

A sence of helplessness engulfed Kate. 'I didn't
mean to frighten you, I was teasing, Debbie,' she
said pleadingly. 'Darling, I wouldn't shake you—I
wouldn't hurt you for the world. Don't look at me
like that, please, dear! You mustn't be frightened of
me.'

Debbie stopped pulling against her, though she still
had the look of a small trapped animal. Kate picked
her up and carried her to the sofa, and Pesky,
jealous, tried to climb up on her lap too. Kate shooed
him away and he pattered off with his tail between
his legs to find consolation in his basket. Kate lifted
Debbie's chin so that she could look into her eyes.
'Debbie, I want you to tell me. Has anybody ever
shaken you—badly, I mean, enough to frighten you?'

The child hesitated, then nodded slowly.

Kate pursed her lips. Who, Lisa? No, not Lisa—
she couldn't believe that of her. 'Who did, dear?
Come along, you must tell me. I promise I'll keep it
a secret.'

'Mrs Borders,' said Debbie finally, in a whisper.

Kate had never heard of Mrs Borders. 'And who is Mrs Borders?' she asked.

'We lived with her before—before Mummy married Simon. We had two rooms in her house, and she looked after me when Mummy was at work.'

'And she wasn't very kind to you?'

Debbie's mouth quivered, and the hand that Kate had taken lay inert. Kate knew it would take all her powers of persuasion to gain the child's confidence.

'Debbie, listen to me, dear. You know I'm a doctor?' An answering nod. 'A doctor has to look after people when they're sick. Sometimes they have a pain in their tummies or their heads and a doctor can give them medicine to make the pain go away. Sometimes they get a different pain—here,' Kate put her hand over her heart. 'It hurts just as much, and though a doctor hasn't got a special medicine for that kind of pain, there *is* a cure. The pain or the ache or the fear of whatever it is that hurts can be made to go away. But anyone with that kind of pain has to help themselves too. They have to talk about it. Just talking about it is a kind of medicine—do you understand?'

'Yes,' said Debbie, and there was something in the tone of her voice that made Kate realise her message had got through.

'Well then, let's talk about this Mrs Borders. I think if you can talk about her you won't be frightened of her any more.'

In broken, not always easy to follow sentences, Kate slowly got the truth. What Debbie couldn't express, Kate's own intuition supplied. On the surface it was a not uncommon story of a middle-aged widow letting off rooms to a mother and child and earning a little extra by looking after the child when the mother was working.

Kate gathered that Lisa had had a better paid job which she gave up when the opportunity to train as a nurse came along. After that Mrs Borders' attitude changed. Perhaps Lisa couldn't afford to pay her as much, or perhaps the woman's health had deteriorated. Both Lisa and Debbie were frightened by her sudden outbursts of temper—but Lisa never knew of the shakings or the slaps or, worse still, the unkind words that had left indelible scars.

'She said I was rubbish,' said Debbie with a sob. 'She said I'd never be anything when I grew up—I was just rubbish.'

Kate felt she'd like a few minutes alone with Mrs Borders and show her what rubbish really was!

'Why didn't you tell your mummy about the way she was unkind to you, and said such wicked things to you?'

'She said if I did she'd turn us both out on the streets and we'd never get anywhere else to live.'

Kate bit back a scathing comment on Mrs Borders with difficulty. Much was clear to her now: Lisa's pathological need to be accepted—Debbie's mistrust of strangers. Mrs Borders had a lot to answer for— and perhaps there had been other Mrs Borders before her whom Debbie was too young to remember, but who had also left invisible scars.

For Kate now the most important thing was to gain this child's trust, and to try to make up to her for her own stupid thoughtlessness.

'How would you like to come on a picnic?' she suggested. 'We'll take Pesky with us and go to a spot I know by the river. You can hold Pesky's lead if you like.'

There's nothing like a little bribery and corruption, thought Kate, seeing how a slow smile suddenly suffused Debbie's thin face. She nodded wordlessly, but followed Kate into the kitchen to watch as some hastily assembled eats were packed into a basket.

Debbie was dressed quite inappropriately for a picnic, but that couldn't be helped. Where other little girls of Debbie's age ran about in play-suits she was in frilly dresses and white knee-length socks. Lisa had the mistaken idea that that showed social status.

Their walk took them slowly and circuitously along Riverside Road, for Pesky, with such a lightweight in tow, made many detours. They went along a path that led to a grassy embankment where part of the river had been dammed to form a small shallow pool safe for children to play in.

The area was packed with families taking advantage of the sudden improvement in the weather. Kate and Debbie had to go way past the pool before they found anywhere to sit. The grass gave way to a shallow cliff with rocky outcrops. Some stone slabs acted very nicely as seats and there was one flat enough to use as a table.

Pesky crept into the shade and lay panting. Kate put out sandwiches, biscuits, crisps and fruit, coffee for herself and fruit juice for Debbie. The child munched away contentedly though in silence as she watched the constant movement of the river. A family of swans glided up, a cob and his pen and four brown cygnets.

Kate wondered what was going through the child's mind, at the same time asking herself how could she ever have thought Debbie plain. There was a gamin appeal about the wistful little face that gave a promise of the handsome young woman to be—the story of the Ugly Duckling all over again.

When they had finished their lunch they threw what was over to the waiting swans. Debbie put so much effort into hurling the left-over sandwiches into the river that Kate had to hang on to her in case she followed suit. They both subsided laughing and Kate felt that at last she had broken down the final barrier between them—she had been accepted. The child's face was flushed with pleasure and she looked at Kate with bashful smiling eyes.

'I like picnics,' she volunteered.

'So do I. We must do it again the next time you come to Yelverthorpe, and we'll ask your mummy and Simon to come too.'

The smile faded instantly. Kate tried coaxing it back. 'Debbie, tell me—why don't you like Simon?'

A slow blush spread across the child's face. The question embarrassed her and she squirmed with discomfiture. But Kate wouldn't give up; she traded on the fact that Debbie now trusted her, even liked her. At last Debbie answered in a voice barely louder than a whisper, 'Now that Mummy's got Simon she won't want me any more, especially if she goes and has another baby. I shall be in the way then.'

'I suppose Mrs Borders told you that,' said Kate in a passion.

'No, we don't see Mrs Borders any more, not since we've moved to the flat. It was a girl at school told me. She said her mummy got married again and her new daddy didn't like her and they sent her away. She lives with her granny now. I haven't got a granny.

Kate wondered how many other children carried this insufferable fear about with them. Judging by the statistics a good many. She slipped her arm around Debbie's thin shoulders and held her close.

'Debbie dear, I must make you understand that Simon will never send you away. He doesn't want to send you away, he wants you to be his friend, he told me so. He's very upset because he thinks you don't like him. I think you could grow to like him very much if you tried. Won't you try—for my sake? For your mummy's sake?'

Tears trembled on Debbie's lashes, then without warning she flung her arms round Kate's neck and burst into racking sobs. This brought Kate near tears herself. There was nothing that made her heart ache more than the crying of an unhappy child.

'Please don't cry, dear, you'll make yourself ill,' she said, pressing the child's wet cheek against her own, yet she knew that this was just the therapy Debbie needed. Better this storm of tears than pent-up fears and resentment.

The sobs gradually ceased, only an occasional shudder marked their passing. Kate took her handkerchief out of her pocket and wiped Debbie's eyes.

'Feel better now?'

Debbie nodded and hiccuped.

'And you're going to give Simon another chance? You will let him be your friend?'

Again Debbie nodded, this time with a ghost of a smile. Then the smile vanished and an anxious look came in its place. 'I want to tell you something, but it might get Mummy into trouble.' Kate had to bend her head to catch the barely audible words.

'Is it about your age?' Some instinct told Kate it was this on the child's mind. 'You're older than six—is that it?'

A short pause, then with a rush, 'I'm nine. I was nine in February.'

Though it was what she had expected, Kate still felt upset by Debbie's answer. She felt hurt to think that Simon had been so easily deceived.

'Why did your mummy make you pretend you're younger than you are?' She didn't like having to

cross-examine the child but felt that the matter had to
come out into the open.

''Cos she didn't want Simon to know how old she
was. She thought he wouldn't marry her if he found
out.' Debbie hung her head, feeling she was betraying
a trust.

Again Kate drew her close. Poor little kid, she had
sacrificed her own peace of mind out of loyalty to her
mother. She could so easily have told Simon the
truth, but she had kept quiet—why? Because she
loved her mother too much to do anything that might
cause her harm?

Kate cupped Debbie's face in her hands and kissed
each tear-stained cheek in turn. Debbie clung to her,
needing all the love she could get. It was an emotional
moment for them both, but it was also a new
beginning to their relationship.

On the walk back Debbie relinquished Pesky's lead
to Kate; she wanted to hold Kate's hand instead.
And she talked—how she talked! Now that she had
found her tongue, it hardly stopped wagging. Kate
realised there were depths to Debbie she hadn't
suspected. For one thing she was highly intelligent. It
couldn't have been easy passing herself off as a child
three years younger than she actually was, yet she
had managed it. Though her small stature was in her
favour, it had taken something extra—and Kate was
beginning to learn what it was: a depth of understanding well beyond her years and a lively imagination.
Many times on that walk Kate glanced down at her
companion with keen amusement, wondering at the
pent-up vitality that was now being released, and also
giving a passing thought to Lisa. Perhaps she too
possessed the same qualities.

That evening, finding herself alone with Lisa, she
took the opportunity to bring up the subject of

Debbie's age. It was painful to watch the way Lisa reacted. She went pale at first, then her cheeks stained crimson. She said falteringly, 'I only lied for Debbie's sake. I wanted to get her away from that awful Mrs Borders. I wanted the chance of a real home.'

'Surely you didn't marry Simon for the sake of a home?' Kate asked incredulously. 'Didn't you love him at all?'

Lisa faced Kate with a mixture of tears and defiance. 'Not at first—no, though I liked him ever so much. He was always so polite and thoughtful towards me, I wasn't used to being treated like that. I knew he was much younger than I was, and I thought at first he was only after the usual thing—knowing I had a child and all. But he wasn't like that. He's the only chap who's ever taken me out and didn't expect anything in return. How could I help but like him? And I love him now, honest to God I do. And I'm going to be a good wife to him, you see if I'm not. I'm going to work hard to get my SRN so that he'll be proud of me. The years won't matter a bit when we're both old—nobody will care tuppence about the difference in our ages then.'

A few tears had escaped and trickled silently down her cheeks, but her pale eyes still blazed defiance. Kate liked her for that. Oh, now she could see what had attracted Simon. There was a simple honesty about Lisa that was as refreshing as it was unusual.

'But now that you love Simon so much should you keep such a secret from him?' she asked gently.

'No I shouldn't, and I feel awful about it—but before we were married, when we were just going out with each other, he was always talking about you, his clever big sister. He sometimes called you his second mother. I thought you were about forty. I had a shock when I found out you were younger than I was. I couldn't face telling him the truth then.'

Kate crumpled up with laughter. She couldn't help herself seeing the look of comic pathos on Lisa's face. She could well imagine Simon boasting about his 'big sister'—he did it with tongue in cheek, but Lisa wasn't to know that.

At first Lisa couldn't understand Kate's untimely hilarity, then she too saw the funny side of it. Suddenly they were both laughing and crying together. 'Please do something for me,' said Lisa, as she wiped her tears away. 'Explain to Simon for me—I haven't got the courage. And another thing,' she plucked nervously at Kate's sleeve, 'I want you to know that I didn't sleep around before I met Simon. It was only the once when I was eighteen—at a party—we'd all had a bit too much to drink, and I never saw the chap again. I can't even remember what he looks like, but I think he must have been something like Simon—kind-hearted and gentle. I suppose I think that because of Debbie. I wouldn't like to think her father wasn't nice.'

Kate smiled a smile of reassurance. 'I think both her father *and* mother must be nice,' she said. Then, 'Come along, the others will be wondering what's keeping us. We're supposed to be going with them to see Mother Shipton's Cave.'

When later, Kate told Simon about Lisa's deception, his eyes crinkled a little with amusement. Otherwise there was no reaction.

'Do you two women take me for a dimwit?' he asked scoffingly. 'I know I'm only twenty' (with heavy irony) 'but I can work some things out for myself! I knew very well Debbie was older than six—I saw some of the books she reads, way above the head of a child that age. Of nine too, come to think of it.

And I knew if Lisa didn't want me to know it was for a very good reason. But I guessed she'd tell me in time. The difference in our ages doesn't make an iota of difference to me, Kate, does it to you?'

'Not now,' Kate admitted honestly. She hesitated, then added, 'I've learnt something this weekend, not only about Lisa but about myself too. I shan't be in such a hurry to judge anyone until I know them in future.'

'And I'll tell you something else, my clever little big sister. In many ways you're a late starter, but you soon catch up!'

When the three of them left for London two days later, Kate found an unexpected void in her life. In some ways she missed Debbie more than she missed the other two. For the past two mornings, as soon as Debbie had heard the alarm go off, she had come running into Kate's room and got into bed with her. How Kate had cherished those few stolen minutes before it was time to get up, and it was during this time she discovered the answer to several things that had puzzled her. Kate now learnt for the first time why Lisa had no relatives. She had been abandoned as a baby and had spent most of her childhood in care.

'That's why I haven't got any aunts and uncles,' Debbie said in the voice of a tragedienne, and before Kate could break in with—'Well, I'm a kind of auntie to you now,' she went on even more dolefully, 'And when I'm grown up and married, my children won't get many Christmas presents or birthday presents because there'll only be me and my husband to give them any, and Mummy of course and Simon, and—and—' she paused, looking questioningly at Kate, who was having some difficulty keeping a straight face.

'You can rely on me, I'll remember to give birthday and Christmas presents to your children,' she promised. 'But don't forget, Debbie, you might have a baby brother or sister before then, and they'll grow up into real aunts or uncles. What a nice lot of relations you'll have then!'

This was a new angle to the idea of her mother having more children and it took a little time to sink in, then a smile like a ray of light spread across Debbie's narrow face. 'I'm glad I belong to a real family now,' she said. She cuddled up against Kate. 'I wish I didn't have to go home tomorrow.'

'Darling, I wish that too.'

Their visit had been a welcome break for Kate in an otherwise uneventful interlude of duties. Audrey Pettifer was away on holiday and Rachel had taken Benjy to visit her mother-in-law. She and her mother-in-law still remained good friends in spite of Matt's defection, and Rachel always took Benjy to see his grandmother in the school holidays. Kate missed her company, and if she had been less busy the days would have dragged.

Kate welcomed the chance to get out on her rounds these warm days of high summer, to her it was the best time of the year. Spring in North Yorkshire could be bitterly cold when sharp east winds blew straight off the hills, and the winter, though beautiful when the moors were blanketed with snow, brought its own problems in the form of bad driving conditions. But August brought scented humid days, bees and butterflies hovering over the late flowers in the valley pastures, carpets of purple heather to feast the eye on, and the gentle sough of the winds in the pines.

When doing her rounds at this time of year Kate often took a packed lunch with her, and when opportunity allowed would make a detour to some quiet beauty spot near a waterfall or tumbling beck. She liked to lie in the heather listening to a chorus of insects. There was no such thing as complete silence in the country, but the sounds were far more harmonious than in town.

At these times her mind always turned to Angus. She had cherished the hope of a letter from him—a card even, at the same time knowing that Angus was the kind of person who would only write if he had something to say. As for sending a picture card—she couldn't imagine him having anything to do with that sort of nonsense!

Martin and Sandra had returned from their honeymoon some time before. There had been a write-up about them in the local paper—'Dr and Mrs Earle are back in Yelverthorpe after an extended honeymoon in Spain. Dr Earle is the resident medical superintendent at The Bays Nursing Home. His father-in-law Mr Desmond Barker, a prominent member of many local societies—etc. etc.' No item of news failed to mention Des Barker some way of the other, and Kate was cynical enough to wonder if he had shares in the newspaper too.

Sandra had once passed her on a stretch of moorland road, driving her father's Mercedes. Kate had a glimpse of bare shoulders, golden skin and gleaming blonde hair, before the car was no more than a speck in the distance. Kate could now think of her and Martin without pain, and with no sense of recrimination. On the contrary she wished them well and hoped Martin had got over the madness that had induced him to ring her from Alicante. She could imagine how Sandra would take it if she ever found out.

One afternoon Kate called in at The Bays to see Miss Self, her one-time patient. Kate had visited her last just after she had been transferred to the nursing home from hospital. She had not recovered from her stroke and nothing more could be done for her now except careful nursing. She was too old and too frail for any form of physiotherapy. That morning Matron had rung Kate to tell her Miss Self's condition was deteriorating, and Kate felt she must go and see her for the last time.

Matron took her up to Miss Self's room herself. The old lady's breathing was laboured and stertorous, it was obvious she was near the end of her life. Fitfully she opened her eyes and as she saw Kate recognition flickered and died again. She struggled to tell them something.

Matron bent to listen. 'It sounds as if she's saying better—but look at her, poor thing—how can she be feeling better?'

But Kate thought she knew what Miss Self was trying to say. 'She doesn't mean better, she means Betty—her old Airedale. She's being cared for in kennels at present. Poor Miss Self, fancy worrying about her dog at a time like this!'

'Well, if that's all the family she has it's understandable,' said Matron in the tone of one who had been through it all before. Her rather autocratic manner belied a warm and caring personality, and Kate liked her even though Matron was inclined to treat her like a member of her junior staff.

Miss Self's breathing grew easier, so faint she could almost be comatose. Matron was called away to see another patient and a nurse came in to sit with the dying woman. There was nothing to keep Kate. She went down the stairs to the entrance hall and had almost reached the outer door when she came face to face with Martin.

They stopped dead a few feet from each other.

There was no embarrassment on Kate's part, but Martin coloured and his eyes couldn't quite meet Kate's. He looked incredibly handsome; the Mediterranean sun had darkened his skin, and that in turn seemed to give his eyes an extra brilliance. Kate waited for the old magic to cast its spell, but it didn't happen.

Instead, for the first time, she saw the weakness in the sweet curve of his mouth, the self-pity in his petulant expression, and she knew she was free of him at last. But at the same time she did not regret the years she had loved him. They had not been wasted—those years had taught her the difference between loving someone and being in love.

'Hallo, Martin, how are you? Did you have a good holiday? You look very fit—beautifully tanned.' She spoke in a clipped manner as if he were no more than an old acquaintance.

Under his tan the blood seeped up and suffused his cheeks again. He seemed to be wrestling with himself as to the best way to answer, then must have decided to play safe.

'You've been to see Miss Self?' His voice was nothing like as steady as hers.

'Yes. I'm afraid she's sinking rapidly now.'

He nodded. 'I knew she was once your patient. That's why I asked Matron to let you know when the end was near.'

'That was kind of you.' Kate made to pass on, but he stepped in front of her.

'Why are you acting like this—why are you so distant?' he demanded in a fierce undertone. 'Why did you hang up on me when I phoned you? I only wanted to talk.'

'It's too late for talking now,' she said, in a tone of one placating a small child. That irritated him. He dropped his eyes and his long dark lashes fanned out on his cheeks like a girl's. 'And please don't make us look so obvious,' she added urgently. Nurses going past were throwing curious glances in their direction.

Martin stepped back out of her way. 'I'm not giving you up, Kate,' he warned her. 'I won't leave you alone.' But she walked on ignoring him, fighting back a hysterical urge to laugh. It wouldn't have been genuine laughter, but then Martin in the rôle of dog in the manger wasn't an amusing spectacle.

CHAPTER NINE

BEFORE the week was out Kate found herself once more in Yelverthorpe church attending another funeral. She sat with Matron, and, glancing around the echoing church, thought how different from last time when it had been packed with mourners. Today there were only six people present to pay their last respects to Miss Self, including Alice McGill sitting on her own at the back. Kate had overheard Dr Barnes telling Derek that the McGills were back in town, so she wasn't surprised to see her.

Afterwards, Alice approached Kate, still dabbing at her eyes. She had cried all through the service.

They exchanged greetings. 'I didn't know you were a friend of Miss Self's,' said Kate.

'Not a friend exactly. I'd just pass the time of day with her if we met in the town.' Alice sniffed and blew her nose. 'Don't think I make a habit of going to funerals. I don't know why I do, they always make me cry. Och now, there I go again!' Alice produced another handkerchief from her bag. 'I've made Angus promise to have me cremated when it's my turn to go. I don't want anybody standing around in the churchyard getting cold on my behalf. Not that we can complain of cold today. So different from when poor Mr Wellbrook was buried.'

'Did you enjoy your holiday?' asked Kate, hoping to bring Angus back into the conversation.

'Weel now, I did and I didn't. I was so worried about Angus most of the time—'

'What's wrong with him?' Kate interrupted with such agitation that Alice looked slightly taken aback.

'There's nothing physically wrong with him—at least I hope not. It's just that there's something on his mind. He seemed to me to be wrestling with some problem. I wish he could have confided in me, but if I said anything about it he just laughed. He was so awfully patient and forbearing all the time we were away, and that's not a good sign with Angus.' Alice sighed and looked vacantly into the middle distance. 'He didn't seem to enjoy his stay in Scotland very much either. He didn't join the shoot once. He used to take Shandy for long walks instead—he said he wanted to be on his own to think. I must say he cheered up considerably our last week and became more sociable. I think he must have come to terms with whatever it was on his mind, but he's not his old self again yet. I long to hear him shouting at me like old times, but he's so polite it's not true! There's something radically wrong with him, Kate, I feel it in my bones. Perhaps he'll improve now he's back in harness. Angus is one of those men who's really only happy when he's working.'

Kate gave Alice a lift back to Damgate, then drove on to see Rachel who had arrived back from Harrogate earlier that day. She parked her car outside the veterinary practice just as Benjy appeared through the arch at the side. He was carrying a kite nearly as large as himself and was escorted by a tall rangy-looking man who adroitly tipped the kite out of the way every time it looked in danger of tripping Benjy up.

The small boy spotted Kate and came running towards her, even hampered as he was.

'Aunty Kate—Aunty Kate!' he cried. 'Look at my new kite! Andrew bought if for me. Andrew's going to show me how to fly it. Andrew's my friend,' he added importantly.

'And Andrew is just about to demonstrate all that he's forgotten about kite-flying.' The man grinned, holding out his hand. 'Hiya, Kate, pleased to meet you.'

Kate liked him on sight. She judged him to be in his middle forties; he had fair hair touched with grey and the widely-spaced eyes she thought of as being peculiar to Americans. His accent was definitely transatlantic. She wondered idly where Rachel had found him and stood watching as man and boy headed up the road towards the park, Benjy's feet drumming rapidly on the pavement in time with the other's long strides.

Kate looked in at the surgery, but only the assistant was there, wiping down the examination table. 'Mrs Wiles is upstairs,' she told her.

Rachel heard Kate coming. 'I'm in my bedroom still unpacking,' she called out.

As soon as Kate set eyes on Rachel she knew something had happened to her. She was struck by the bloom that seemed to radiate from her friend's face. 'I sense romance in the air,' she said, as they kissed. 'Who's the tall fair stranger in your life?'

'Don't be arch, Kate—it doesn't suit you,' but Rachel couldn't suppress a certain inner satisfaction. She shook out a dress before putting it on a hanger, at the same time giving Kate a provocative smile. 'His name is Andrew Birch and I met him at Linda's.' (Linda was her mother-in-law.) 'Andrew's mother is an old friend of Linda, she was a GI bride—one of the first, in fact, and Linda was her bridesmaid. Now Andrew is on a year's sabbatical at London University, he's something to do with electronics, and spending some of his vacation at Harrogate. If you ask me I think Linda engineered our meeting.' Rachel chewed her bottom lip thoughtfully. 'Linda thinks it's high time I got Matt out of my system.'

'I'm with her there,' put in Kate.

Rachel went on as if Kate hadn't spoken, 'I believe Linda and Andrew's mother plotted something between them. Andrew's marriage went on the rocks about two years ago—that's partly why he came over to England—at his mother's suggestion!—to help him forget. Oh, Kate, I never thought I could ever love again after Matt, but as soon as I met Andrew, well—I'm not going to say it was love at first sight, that's too corny—but by golly, it was very near it!' Her dark eyes were luminous with joy giving Kate an insight into how much Andrew meant to her.

Kate was glad for Rachel. She considered she had been carrying the torch for her ex-husband too long already—but, in a way, she was envious too. Anybody who could look as Rachel looked now was experiencing unalloyed happiness, something Kate hadn't felt for a long time.

She didn't realised she had sighed aloud until Rachel said, 'What is it, Kate? You're not still mooning after Martin, are you?'

'Of course not. He's out of my system now just as much as Matt is out of yours.'

'Is it Angus, then?' Kate was startled by Rachel's frankness, alarmed too at her perspicacity.

She began to bluster. 'I haven't seen him since before he went on holiday. I don't know anything about Angus.'

'Oh Kate, who are you trying to fool? Me or yourself?' Rachel pushed her clothes to one side and pulled Kate on to the bed beside her. 'I had my suspicions before, now they're certainties. Perhaps being in love myself has made it easier for me to recognise it in others. I saw the giveaway look in your eyes when you said his name. Why try to hide it—be proud! I'm proud of loving Andrew.'

'Because he loves you in return—that's obvious.' Kate sprang to her feet and began to pace the narrow strip of carpet between the bed and the wardrobe. Rachel, watching her, thought, 'Why, how attractive she is—I've never seen her so attractive-looking,' but it was a beauty borrowed from despair rather than joy. The darkened skin beneath Kate's eyes enhanced the golden flecks in her irises, and helped to emphasise the eyes' unusual shape. Her recent loss of weight made her cheekbones more prominent, giving her face the hollowed sculptured appearance of a professional model. Her bright reddish-gold hair appeared to drain the colour from her cheeks, and her pallor was made even more noticeable by the dark dress she was wearing. Rachel remembered then that Kate had just come from Miss Self's funeral, it was one of the first bits of news she had heard on reaching home again. Impatient with herself for forgetting, she said apologetically,

'Sorry, Kate, for ranting on at you, I'd forgotton about the funeral. Could you manage a cup of coffee? I could do with one myself.'

'I can't stay—I'm due back at the surgery—'

'I won't detain you ten minutes.'

Over coffee they discussed Betty, Miss Self's old Airedale. There was no question of her being moved, she was quite at home in the kennels out in the yard. 'It won't be long before she follows her mistress,' said Rachel, staring thoughtfully into her cup. 'Did you know Miss Self had left provision for her in her will? She left most of her money to charity. Would you believe she hadn't a single relative and she'd outlived all her friends?'

It *was* easy to believe, thought Kate, remembering the empty church.

Before she let her go Rachel brought up the subject of Angus once more. 'Nothing personal this time,' she promised. 'I can see it distresses you to talk about him, though I can't think why. What I wanted to ask is, did Alice say anything about him? About his health, I mean? Only Dad mentioned to me before I went to Harrogate that he thought Angus was acting a bit odd at times.'

Kate nodded. 'Alice seems to think there's something on his mind—'

'Perhaps it's you,' Rachel broke in, then looked apologetic again when she saw the effect her words had on Kate. 'Sorry, I'd forgotten you were so touchy about him.'

'Look, Rachel, let's get this straight—I'm not touchy about Angus, I'm just realistic. I mean no more than *that*—' lost for the right word, Kate snapped her fingers instead, 'as far as Angus is concerned. If he has anything on his mind it has nothing to do with me, I can assure you. Now I must get back to the surgery—thanks for the coffee.'

She almost ran down the stairs, her eyes blurred with tears she didn't want Rachel to see. She got into her car, slammed into gear and drove jerkily the short distance to the practice, then turning into the narrow space allotted for parking, she collided with a post and heard a crump of damaged metal—she had dented her nearside wing. It was the last straw. She dropped her head on the steering wheel and let all her pent-up feelings flow out as tears. She certainly felt better for it—that was until she raised her head again and saw Dr Barnes on the pathway watching her in consternation.

The sight of his young assistant curled up in her car crying her eyes out affected Dr Barnes deeply. He didn't enjoy his evening meal at all. It couldn't be anything to do with work, he decided—she had no problems with that and was very popular with the patients. No, she needed a holiday, that's what it was—just lately he'd noticed a dulling of her spirits, a lack of her usual fire, and he must do something about it. Nobody was going to accuse him of overworking his staff!

He summoned Kate to his room the following morning and cross-examined her about her holiday arrangements, and on discovering she had not yet made any plans asked if she had any preference.

Kate told him no, but didn't add that at the moment she couldn't feel any enthusiasm for going anywhere. Dr Barnes gave her a shrewd look. 'Then perhaps you'll allow me to recommend a little place on the coast near Robin Hood's Bay. You'll be well looked after there,' and he was jotting down the address for her when the phone at his elbow shrilled.

'Hallo—Oh, hallo, Bill yes, what is it?' he answered in his genial way. Then his expression changed and he stared blankly in Kate's direction. 'Oh, my God, how did it happen?' He listened, his mouth open slightly. 'Of course—of course. Is McGill dealing with it? Poor devil—his own sister! Keep me informed, won't you?' He replaced the receiver.

Kate's mouth had gone dry. 'Has anything happened to Alice McGill?' she asked anxiously.

Dr Barnes blinked and brought her face into focus. 'I'm afraid she's suffered a terrible injury. Apparently she tripped and fell down the cellar steps and struck the bridge of her nose on the edge of the last step. Dr Goodwin says her face is badly fractured. She's in hospital now and her brother is operating on her shortly, and Bill Goodwin is to administer the anaesthetic. That's why he phoned—to tell me he wouldn't be able to play a round of golf we'd planned for this afternoon.'

A temporary giddiness overcame Kate and she leant on the desk for support. Alice—dear kind Alice, with her warm grey eyes and ready smile. 'Could you spare me, Dr Barnes?' she asked him. 'I would like to go along to the hospital to see if I can help.'

'She's in capable hands—her brother's and Dr Goodwin's.'

Dr Goodwin was the senior anaesthetist at the District Hospital and Kate had done most of her training under him.

'I mean as a friend,' Kate explained. 'I—when Alice comes round I'd like to be there.'

Dr Barnes understood. He was concerned about Kate, she took things too much to heart. She had lost what little colour she had and he could see her lips trembling. He hoped a holiday would put her back on her feet. She was a willing little worker, and they all took advantage of that.

'Yes, run along,' he said kindly. 'I can look after your patients as I won't be taking this afternoon off now, and I dare say Goodwin will welcome an extra pair of hands.'

Kate came face to face with Dr Goodwin in the corridor of the dental block. Obviously Dr Barnes had phoned back to him, because he showed no surprise at seeing her.

'Glad you could come over,' he said. 'You can do the fetching and carrying for me. She's got some really nasty facial injuries—and just from tumbling down a flight of steps! It's said that some of the worst injuries occur in the home. I'll believe it after this.'

'What—what are the injuries exactly?' asked Kate.

'Both zygomas are broken and the maxilla has separated from the base of the skull, but remarkably her eyesight is not affected, except for the immediate result of haemorrhage. She's unable to close her mouth because the maxilla has dropped and the upper teeth have come down to meet the lower.'

Kate closed her eyes, visualising the extent of Alice's suffering. 'When did this happen?' she asked tremulously.

'Late last night. Thank God Mr McGill was in the house and he got her into hospital right away. First priority was life-saving measures—drip to restore lost fluid, blood tests for blood transfusion, establishment and maintenance of adequate airways.' Dr Goodwin looked not unhopeful. 'It's going to be a long and demanding operation to put Alice McGill's face together again—but it can be done. Mr McGill and the plastic surgeons between them will win this battle. I'm just off to the anaesthetic room now. You can start scrubbing up any time, Kate.'

News had quickly got round about the operation and both dental and medic house officers were in the theatre anxious to see Angus at work. Kate took her place by the anaesthetic machine, and after making sure that all was well with his patient, Dr Goodwin joined her. Then Angus stepped up to the operating table. From where Kate was standing she couldn't see Alice's face all that clearly, but she didn't mind that as long as she could watch Angus—his hands said everything.

He paused and looked round at the array of masked faces. For an instant his eyes rested on Kate's, the dark blue irises reflecting what could have been a smile of recognition. She felt he was pleased to see her, she even imagined she saw a flicker of approval, then he became the surgeon once more with a difficult task in hand and juniors waiting for instruction. Kate wondered what it must be like for him knowing that it was his sister lying there on the operating table. Could he really be as detached as he appeared?

'Ladies and gentlemen,' he began, his voice brisk, completely unemotional—but Kate could sense the anxiety underlying his words. 'In the first instance this operation will entail the removal of small fragments of bone, in conserving the nerves and blood vessels, then repositioning the maxilla.'

He was handed a pair of large stainless steel forceps about fourteen inches long and designed to grip large pieces of bone. Repositioning in this case meant pulling the maxilla (upper jaw) slightly forward and manipulating it upward so that the broken ends of the bones were in contact with the checkbones (zygomas). Kate was fascinated, watching the swiftness and facility with which he made this insuperable task, to her, look so easy.

Once he had repositioned the face bones not only to his satisfaction but also to the satisfaction of the consultant plastic surgeon, who was also present, Angus proceeded with the next step of the operation; that was to insert rods into the plaster of Paris skullcap that had previously been fitted to the patient's head.

'It will be important to maintain the maxilla in position for several weeks,' he said. His voice was at variance with the strain that was beginning to show in his eyes and Kate could see perspiration breaking out on his forehead. 'This will be done by inserting rods with threaded ends into a couple of places in the maxilla and by the use of clamps fixing them to the rods in the plaster of Paris skullcap. While I'm doing this would anybody like to ask questions?'

Someone at the back asked, 'Will the plastic surgeons take over while the rods are still in position?'

'I think Mr Coleman could answer that one, but as I'm the one in the hot seat I'll do it for him.' This touch of levity combined with the knowledge that the major part of the operation had been conluded successfully lessened the tension that had been slowly building up. The fact that the patient was Angus's sister and had sustained such horrifying injuries had added a dramatic twist to the situation. He continued, 'No, plastic surgery isn't feasible until the bones of the face are completely set, that is in about six to eight weeks, then the plastic surgeon's task will be to restore the nose and tidy up the skin.'

'Will the patient be able to speak or eat during that time?' asked someone else.

'Fortunately the mandible wasn't fractured, so when she is sufficiently recovered the patient will be able to communicate, not easily, but sufficiently to make herself understood, and to take liquid nourishment.' Angus paused. 'My sister is lucky to be alive,' he said, for the first time referring to Alice other than as the patient. 'And extremely lucky not to have lost one or both eyes.'

He peeled off his gloves and slipped down his mask, and it became plain to them all then that he wasn't as impassive as he appeared. There was a nervous twitch at the corner of his mouth and the skin around his eyes was white with exertion. He flexed his fingers several times, then stared at his hands with a look of such despair that Kate had a sudden feeling of hopelessness. What could she do to comfort him—to assure him that he had done

everything in his power to save Alice's face? Not that
Angus gave anybody the chance to congratulate him.
To everyone's surprise he turned and strode swiftly
out of the theatre.

Dr Goodwin watched him with worried eyes, then
told Kate to take over. 'I'm going after Mr McGill—
he looks all in. It's been more of a strain than he
bargained for,' and off he went too, giving her no
chance to ask for further instructions.

Alice was practically unrecognisable beneath the
steel framework that was holding her face together.
Kate went through the usual routine of checking her
pulse and blood pressure and looking into the eyes to
see that the pupils were normal. The Theatre Sister
and her team of nurses had already started to clean
up and the theatre porters were approaching to wheel
the patient to the recovery room where Kate could
leave her in the charge of the staff nurse.

For the present there was nothing more Kate could
do. She knew Dr Goodwin would be back shortly to
have another look at Alice. She had already disposed
of her theatre gown, gloves and mask, now she went
to the cloakroom to wash and tidy up. She had left
her handbag in her car and couldn't renew her make-
up, she hadn't even a comb with her to run through
her hair, so she smoothed it as best as she could with
her fingers. What does it matter how you look, she
told herself, think of poor Alice.

She met Dr Goodwin again in the main corridor.
'How is Mr McGill?' she enquired.

'Better—much better,' but Kate didn't take much
comfort from that. Dr Goodwin was still looking too
concerned. 'He didn't get much sleep last night, that's
his main problem, I believe—that's what he says,
anyway. He wants to see you in his room,' he added,
then before she ran off, 'How is our patient?'

Kate was impatient to get to Angus. 'No cause for concern. Her colour is returning and her pulse is strong.'

'Good, good—but I'd better check up for myself. Tell Mr McGill I'll give him a buzz as soon as his sister regains consciousness.'

Kate tapped on the door of Angus's room and as there was no answer went in. Angus was standing staring out of the window. Even his back showed the pressure he was under, the broad shoulders sagged. 'Angus,' she said softly.

He turned. The white lines of fatigue round his eyes had spread to nose and mouth, yet he managed an apology for a smile. As for Kate, at any other time she would have been taken aback by his appearance. He had discarded his theatre gown and she saw he was wearing a well-fitting pale blue short-sleeved jacket over matching trousers. In different circumstances she would have remarked upon it, even now her expression showed her surprise, for Angus said, trying to sound jaunty,

'How do you like my new image? It was meant as a morale-booster, but I'm afraid I didn't time it right. My morale had a bashing instead of a boost.' The jauntiness in his voice turned to self-mocking bitterness, and she could have wept for him.

Then more calmly he went on, 'I hope Bill Goodwin didn't give you the impression I wanted you for something urgent—it was just to let you know how I appreciated you coming along. I know it isn't your day for visiting the hospital, so you must have come specially, and I want to thank you on Alice's behalf. You're a loyal little pal.'

Always a pal or a friend, Kate thought wistfully— nothing more than that. She stole a look at him, but he was staring past her, looking unseeingly into the distance with such a look of quiet rage in his eyes that she wondered if he was inwardly cursing fate for what had happened to his sister.

Again she had to keep a hold on herself, the urge to offer sympathy was so strong. But could she trust herself to stop at sympathy? Might she not reveal other secret longings too? She still clung perilously to the formality she called her pride.

'May I see Alice when she's recovered consciousness?' she asked, and was surprised, and not a little hurt when he refused this request.

'I'm putting an embargo on any visitors until the bones have knitted together. It's still touch and go and I can't afford to take the slightest risk. You wouldn't want Alice to be scarred for the rest of her life, would you?'

'Of course not! But—'

'I know what you're about to say—you're staff, not a visitor, but you're also Alice's friend. She'd try to talk—she'd be sure to cry, you know what she's like. I'm sorry, Kate, you'll have to be patient.' He gave a poor substitute for one of his old wolfish grins. 'And I know how hard it is for you of all people to be patient.'

She tried to smile back. 'I'm going on holiday in two weeks' time. Can't I see her before then?'

He considered, then shook his head. 'Best not—but there's nothing to stop you writing. She'll be pleased to receive letters. And I hope you have a very enjoyable holiday—I expect you're ready for it.'

Kate felt she was being dismissed. Angus didn't even ask her where she was planning to spend her holiday. There seemed to be an invisible barrier between them and they stood either side of it, saying the right things, being polite to each other, but hiding what was in their hearts. At least that was how *she* felt—she couldn't speak for Angus, but she knew he was hiding something.

He followed her to the door. 'Kate!' Her hand was on the door handle, but she paused, struck by the note of urgency in his voice. Her heart skipped a beat—perhaps—oh, dear Lord, let him say he wanted to see her again!

'Yes?' She turned hopefully.

He came close, looking at her with intense eyes. 'I must clear up something before you go—to apologise for my behaviour lately. First of all my outburst in the churchyard—I hope you didn't take it personally. I was a bit wrought-up that day, but that's no excuse. But my worst sin was my boorish behaviour that time on our trip back from York—'

She tried to stop him, she didn't want to hear any more, her heart began to knock against her ribs and a vein in her throat began throbbing.

'No, you must let me finish,' he insisted. 'I said things I didn't mean because something you said to me stung my stupid pride. I had no right to criticise you because of Martin Earle; what goes on between you two is no business of mine. And I took advantage of you too, for that I'm deeply sorry. I didn't stop to think you might find my behaviour offensive. The only excuse I have is that the magic of that evening sent me temporarily out of my mind.' He laughed, but his eyes were solemn. They held an expression that haunted her for days afterwards—of someone beyond hope. In a man like Angus McGill with his self-assurance and masterly command of any situation, it was pitiful to see. 'I'm making a hash of this apology. As you know, apologies are not in my line.' His false jocularity jarred. 'I—that is, both Alice and I value your friendship; we wouldn't want to lose you because of my stupidity.'

Kate stood there with a smile pinned to her face like a badge for valour, going through the motions of assuring him he had nothing to reprove himself for, said her goodbyes and escaped. Only when she was safe in her car did she allow her feelings to give way to despair. Not in tears—she was past tears—but in an icy calm. Again that word friendship—it daunted her with its suggestion of a lost cause. She struggled to regain some of her old optimism. Friendship was a small consolation for love, but it was better than nothing.

CHAPTER TEN

THE drive to Robin Hood's Bay took Kate across lonely moorland roads where signs of autumn were already showing in the coppery tones of ferns and trees. In the distance, mist hung like gossamer on the high hills, but the sky above was a brilliant blue. Kate loved autumn, she usually felt at her best then—but not this year.

Engraved on her mind was an image of Angus as she had last seen him—hollowed-eyed and weary but putting on a front of wit and bonhomie. He had said nothing about seeing her again, had made no effort to get in touch before she left for Robin Hood's Bay.

Then disquieting rumours about him began to filter through the medical pipeline. Though he still attended the hospital for his outpatients' clinic and to instruct his students he had passed all operations over to his senior registrar. Conjecture was rife. Some said that the tremendous effort he had put into repairing his sister's face had been his 'swan song', that he intended to give up surgery altogether, but this was discounted as unfounded rumour. Kate couldn't help recalling Alice's confidences in her in Yelverthorpe churchyard—her conviction that there was something on her brother's mind. Though she seemed to think at the time that any problem had been resolved. But had it? That was what had niggled Kate, and the doubt was still niggling now as she followed the road that snaked across the moors.

She had left Yelverthorpe determined to enjoy her holiday, but it was going to be hard work getting in the right mood. She was even beginning to regret leaving Pesky behind, at least he would have been company for her, but Rachel had advised against taking him and had offered to look after him for the two weeks Kate would be away.

On Friday when she had been walking Pesky along to Rachel's, Kate saw Martin for the first time since their encounter at The Bays. He was just about to draw away from the kerbside; he saw her too but pretended he hadn't, and there was something guilty and furtive about the way he shot past her in his new car. It was the sort of car he had hankered after in his student days—was it a bribe from his father-in-law? A hidden reminder of what Martin had to lose if he played fast and loose with Des Barker's daughter? It was all conjecture, but it could account for the fact that Martin had not fulfilled his threat not to leave her alone. She was woman enough to have felt hurt for a moment or two—then had laughed the matter off. After all, knowing Martin, how could she expect to compete with a Porsche!

Kate had hoped that in spite of Angus's embargo she would be allowed to see Alice before going away, but she couldn't get past the ward Sister, who had no intention of disobeying the chief. Kate sent in books and flowers instead and had received a letter written in a shaky hand in return:

Dear Kate,

Angus told me you helped at my operation. Thank you, dear child, for bothering about a stupid woman who doesn't look where she's going. Angus is pleased with my progress, though personally

I shall be pleased to get rid of this contraption round my face! It must make me look like something from outer space. Angus said I might finish up with a longer face than I had originally, but I think he's only saying that out of charity, knowing how I was always moaning about my face looking so square. Now I'm being punished for my vanity, and serve me right! Angus said he thought you looked rather wan, so take care of yourself and have a lovely holiday.

Love,

Alice McGill

Kate had smiled wryly over the word wan—surely the understatement of the year—or else she was better at disguising her feelings than she thought.

She reached Robin Hood's Bay in the early afternoon, stopping her car at the top of a hill to look down on the village nestling at the water's edge. The main street tipped precipitously downwards and ended in a slipway that now at high tide was awash with waves. Either side of the street, the stone cottages, once the homes of generations of fishermen, glowed warmly in the afternoon sun. Dr Barnes's instructions had been to take the first road north out of Robin Hood's Bay and three miles further on she would find Gibraltar House along a private lane and overlooking a sheltered stretch of beach.

Gibraltar House turned out to be a square, solid-looking residence that had been built in Nelson's time by a naval commander. It was now a private hotel and Mrs Harker, the proprietress, herself took Kate to her room. Considering that the reputation of her establishment was founded on its traditional Yorkshire home cooking she didn't bat an eyelid when Kate said she was a vegetarian. Kate had the feeling she would have received the same calm, smiling response if she had announced that she only ate raw fish.

'In that case I'll have to rise to the occasion,' she said, with just a hint of a North Country accent—and rise to the occasion she did!

Kate would have been the first to admit that she was an unadventurous cook, she hadn't the time to experiment, so her mealtimes at Gibraltar House became events to look forward to. Tomatoes as big as saucers and stuffed with smoked cheese and herbs, spiced potatoes tossed in coconut—cucumber and date salad with yogurt dressing—ratatouille and nut cutlets—there was no end to the variety of dishes. And every dinner ended with a genuine Wensleydale cheese. Mrs Harker would have no truck with factory made cheeses, hers came direct from the farm.

Under the influence of sea air, effortless days and good food, Kate quickly began to look and feel better. Most of the other guests were older than she was, among them two ladies so incredibly alike Kate took them for sisters and then discovered they were sisters-in-law—a Mrs and Miss Beacon. Another regular guest had been in the RAF during the war and still clung to the rôle of a one-time fighter pilot. He sported a handlebar moustache, wore cravats instead of ties, and flirted outrageously with the two Belisha Beacons, as he called them—a joke completely lost on Kate until it was explained to her that that had been the original name of the beacons marking the pedestrian crossings first introduced during 1935 and named after the then Minister of Transport, Hore-Belisha.

But where her elderly companions were quite content to sit in the lounge or on the verandah that overlooked the sea, Kate wanted to be out and about, and those leisurely days of exploration in her little car turned out to be the highlights of her holiday.

She discovered other delightful little fishing villages along that stretch of coastline, little gems from an historic past—like Runswick Bay and Staithes which shared with Robin Hood's Bay the same old-world charm. They offered an elusive glimpse of another age when the fishermen went out in their cobles to collect crabs and their womenfolk walked the tiny alleys between the houses wearing the traditional bonnets still obtainable from Staithes but now bought only as souvenirs. Kate bought one to send to Debbie. 'This is what I shall wear when I'm a great-aunt to your children,' she wrote.

The bracken was beginning to rust over as October approached, but there were still bright patches of heather about. Kate picked a sprig for luck. Though not superstitious she wasn't above giving fate a nudge. It was that same day that on her return to the hotel during the afternoon she saw Angus's car parked in the drive.

Squadron-Leader Foss was standing looking at it with expressions of envy and delight and admiration flitting across his weathered face. Hearing Kate draw up he looked across at her, and spread his hands in a gesture of resignation. 'What a sight for sore eyes!' he remarked, his voice full of reverence. 'It takes me back to the good old days— *my* young days. Lucky, lucky man who owns this car!'

No, I'm the lucky one, thought Kate. Had the sprig of heather had anything to do with it?—but she quickly dismissed that idea as foolish. She hurried into the hotel and was accosted by Mrs Harker as she ran towards the staircase. 'Oh, there you are, Dr Murray. You have a visitor—he left a message to say he'd wait for you on the beach. He thought it too fine a day to stay indoors. Will he be staying for dinner?'

'I really don't know—' Kate hadn't thought as far ahead as that. It was just sufficient for the moment to know that Angus was here—had come especially to see her. 'Anyway, he loves steak,' she added, knowing that Mrs Harker couldn't go wrong with that.

But she wasn't allowed to escape so easily—the two Beacon ladies had been hovering, waiting to speak to her. 'Dr Murray, I've been so hoping for a word with you—' it was Miss Beacon, and she was holding her side. 'I've got this funny little pain here and I just wondered—'

This was not the first time that Miss and Mrs Beacon had just wondered about odd and fleeting pains since finding out that Kate was a doctor, and usually Kate had only been too ready to put their minds at rest. But now she was impatient to get changed and join Angus. She made her excuses as tactfully as she could, and though disappointed, the two ladies were obviously curious. As she reached the bend in the stairs she overheard Mrs Beacon ask of Mrs Harker, 'Was that splendid-looking man with the reddish hair and charming smile the one Dr Murray was talking about?'

Splendid looking and charming? Yes—she couldn't have chosen better words to describe him herself. There *was* something splendid about Angus's leonine brow and he had all the charm of a Don Juan when he cared to use it.

Kate knew just what she wanted to change into— the new pink cotton trousers and the white silk shirt blouse that gleamed like silver in certain lights. She had been keeping them for a special occasion, and what could be more special than this! A wide black patent-leather belt gave the finishing touch to her

outfit, that and her black beads and the jet earrings
she had purchased on a visit to Whitby the day
before. Whitby was renowned for its jet. She looked
at herself in the mirror. Not really suitable attire for
the beach, but what did that matter?—she wanted to
look her best for Angus, and she knew she *was*
looking her best. The bloom had returned to her
cheeks and her eyes had regained their old lustre.

The beaches along that coastline were a popular
attraction to holidaymakers. The sand was soft and
wàrm to the feet, the water crystal-clear, and the
pebbles with subtle colorations were much sought
after by amateur geologists. Kate had collected some
to take back for Benjy, but few treasure-seekers
ventured as far as Gibraltar Bay. It was guarded both
ends by outcrops of rock as high as houses and the
only way down was through the garden of the hotel,
and then by the unfenced zigzagging cliff path.

She spotted Angus long before he was aware of her
approach. He had on the well-cut lightweight suit he
had been wearing for their visit to York, but
unmindful of the sand or the salt spray he had seated
himself near the water's edge, his knees up to his
chin and his arms locked round them, staring lazily
out to sea. Kate could only see his profile, but his
whole attitude struck her as that of a man at peace
with himself and the world, and she marvelled at the
difference in him since she last saw him. But then,
once before when he had had an attack of malaria,
he had amazed her by his remarkable powers of
recovery.

Angus looked round, then saw her and got easily
to his feet. 'You're looking much fitter,' he greeted
her, but no words of love could have given her
greater joy. He was obviously pleased to see her.

'You're looking pretty fit yourself,' she retorted

lightly, but it wasn't lightly meant. He *was* looking well, he even appeared to have regained the few pounds he had lost. His eyes sparkled in their old menacing, mischievous manner sending an excited awareness coursing over her.

'Is that your paddling attire?' he teased, and matching her mood to his she came back with, 'No, this is my sitting-on-the-beach-talking outfit.'

As if something about her facetious words had struck some sober chord, his expression changed, grew solemn. He said, 'Yes, that's why I've come—to talk. I have something to discuss with you, Kate. Is there anywhere private we can go?'

A cloud passed over the sun just then, but it wasn't that that made Kate shiver. She felt a sudden portent that Angus was going to reveal something discomfiting.

'What could be more private than here?' she asked, spreading her arms wide—embracing the beach and the cliffs. She spoke flippantly, hoping to jostle Angus away from earnestness—to stop him saying that which she didn't wish to hear. 'Sorry I didn't bring a couple of deck-chairs with me, but I couldn't get them under my arm.'

'No more joking, Kate, this is serious.' Angus's manner was brusque now, even purposeful. 'We'll stay here by all means, but if you want somewhere to sit—well, come over here.'

He propelled her unceremoniously towards the boulders where natural perches had been carved out of the rocks by centuries of weathering. The sea shimmered like shot silk under an azure sky and gulls circled raucously overhead. It was a romantic setting, but all thoughts of romance had fled from Kate's heart, she felt too intimidated.

He found her a ledge that made a comfortable seat but remained standing himself, towering over her blocking out the sun, his face cast in shadow. The sun behind him created a bright aureole of his hair, and made his eyes appear as sightless caverns. But Kate was only too aware that he was watching her intently. Again she shivered.

'Are you cold, Kate?' Angus asked in surprise.

'No, just apprehensive.'

'Why should you be apprehensive?' this time showing no surprise.

'Because you sounded very ominous when you said you had something to discuss with me.'

He gave a low grunt that could have been assent or one of his odd chuckles. She heard him rattle the change in his pocket. 'All right, no beating about the bush—I'll tell you straight out. I'm going to give up oral surgery, instead I'm negotiating to buy the old Watson house; you know, that great old mausoleum just out of town that's been empty for a year? I'm planning to turn it into a clinic—'

The first thing that came to Kate's mind was that it was the story of Martin and The Bays all over again. With the increase in an ageing population there was a great demand for private nursing homes. It was a blow that completely unhinged her, and she stared at him with baffled, angry eyes.

'And private, of course!' she said accusingly.

He was nonplussed by her reaction. 'Well, yes, I shall be financing it initially, but once it's established I intend to put in for a government grant, and then—'

But Kate gave him no chance to finish his explanation. She jumped to her feet, quivering with emotion. 'You're no better than a money-grabber!' she stormed. 'I suppose the pickings are easier in a private nursing home than in an NHS hospital! Oh, I'm so disappointed in you—' Her words came pouring out heedlessly. 'I was so proud of you—so full of admiration for your work. I remember watching your hands, thinking how adept you were at even the most intricate operation—the most fiddly task. How you can give all that up to run a potty little private nursing home I just don't understand—'

'Shut up—or I'll shut you up!' He came at her like an angry bull, and she backed away, thinking he was going to strike her. His eyes had a wild, frenzied look about them and his face was pale with anger. Then at the last minute he controlled himself and gave her a stare that made her feel about two inches high. The grimness of his expression relaxed a little and his lips curved upwards, but it was more a grinning mask that confronted her than a human face.

'You can be as sweet as a kitten one minute, then you suddenly unsheath your claws and turn into a wildcat,' he said with a tinge of bitterness. 'Ah, Dr Murray, what a disappointment you are to me too! I thought I could speak to you as one colleague to another—I came for advice and encouragement. But you pre-judged me before I had a chance to explain.' He shrugged. 'So what's the point in trying to explain now? We'll never be on the same wavelength, you and I—we live entirely different lives. Yours is all cut and dried, everything black or white—whereas most of the time, lately anyway, I seemed to be going about in a grey fog.' He interrupted himself with a curt, unamused laugh. 'Well, no longer. I've found my way out of the fog at last, and that's what I wanted to talk to you about. But it's too late now. You wouldn't be interested.'

Most of what he was saying was unintelligible to Kate, but she could understand that she had hurt him even more deeply than he had hurt her. She regretted the mad impulse that had made her break in on his explanation. Now she wanted to hear what he had to say, she *wanted* his confidence—but she had lost it. One look at his steely eyes was sufficient to show her there could be no second chance.

'I suppose you won't be staying for dinner now,' she said dully—really for the want of anything else to say, and that *did* make him laugh. He threw back his head and gave one loud bellow that was almost like a cry for help.

'Oh, Kate, that's rich! You mincing little madam—you shatter my dreams, then regret I won't be staying to dinner. Have a heart, do you really think I can indulge in small talk amid the faded elegance of your hotel? No, this is goodbye—truly goodbye this time, but I won't go without leaving you something to remember me by,' and taking her unawares, he pulled her roughly into his arms, pressed his mouth against hers, forced her lips apart, and gave her a kiss as insulting as it was passionless.

She watched him walk away, the back of her hand pressed against her mouth, trying to resurrect all the old hatred she had once felt for him. But it was no good—she loved him, and now she had lost him.

The guests at Gibraltar House wondered what had come over their charming Dr Murray. Two days ago she had been such a lively companion, but since then she had withdrawn into her shell, appearing only at mealtimes. Had it anything to do with the visit of that large redheaded man? Strange that he hadn't stayed for dinner that day—stranger still that Dr Murray herself didn't appear either.

Kate toyed with the breakfast that had just been

placed before her, glad that there was only one more day of her holiday to get through. She was looking forward to getting back to work—to coping with other people's problems rather than brooding on her own.

The post had arrived. Mrs Harker's son Tom brought in two letters for Kate, one from Simon and the other from Alice. She opened Simon's first, but he had only addressed the envelope. The missive inside was from Debbie.

> Dear Kate,
>
>   Thank you for the bonnet. Simon says it makes me look like a milkmade. Simon had bought me some new cloathes, a track-suit and some jeans and two swett shirts. Simon took me to the science museum (Simon told me how to spell science). It was a bit boreing, but I liked it. I got into trouble at school. My teacher asked me what I wanted to be when I grew up and I said a vegetarian (Simon again, thought Kate) and she made me stay in during break cause she said I was cheeky. But I wasn't being cheeky, I just want to be like you. Will you come and stay with us at half-term? Mummy said to ask you.
>
>   Lots of love,
>
>   Debbie xxxx

For the first time in two days Kate smiled. It was obvious Simon had won Debbie over. You sly one, she thought—you got round her with presents and flattery. But she knew it went deeper than that.

Alice's letter was a long one and in a much steadier hand than her first attempt.

Dear Kate,

        I know Angus was driving over to see you yesterday, but I haven't seen him today yet to ask him how he got on. What do you think of his news? Don't you think he's marvellous the way he's come fighting back after such a devastating blow (blow? what blow?—Kate felt a sickening lurch in the pit of her stomach)? I told you there was something on his mind when we were in Scotland. If only I'd known what it was then I might have been able to comfort him, but that's my brother all over. Keeps his troubles to himself and only shares his joys.

    I can only imagine what he must have gone through when the rheumatologist confirmed his suspicion that he was suffering from rheumatoid arthritis and would eventually have to give up surgery. (The words seemed to jump off the paper and dance in the air before Kate's horrified eyes, she gripped the page until her knuckles whitened.) Don't you think it a cruel twist of fate that a man like Angus should lose the use of his hands?' Kate gave an audible gasp and Miss Beacon looked across at her anxiously. 'But since he thought of this wonderful idea of buying the old Watson place and converting it into a kind of clinic to help others with the same complaint he's been like a man reborn.

    He looked so happy yesterday when he called to see me and said he was going to tell you all about his plans. I'm longing to know what you think. He needs encouraging, Kate. He looks strong, but he's got a very soft centre and is easily hurt. You know what I fondly wish for you two, don't you—perhaps by now it has come to pass. I could go on writing at length, but Sister is frowning at me, and in any case I suspect this is old news to you by now.

In hospital jargon, I'm doing as well as can be expected! Actually I feel fine, but looking forward to getting back to my own bed.

Love,

Alice.

Kate walked woodenly out of the dining-room and across the hall to the phone booth, and dialled the number of the Yelverthorpe animal surgery. Rachel herself answered the phone.

'Kate!—you've just caught me, I'm off to York for the day, with Andrew and Benjy. We're taking a holiday as Andrew has to return to London next week, and we promised Benjy to take him to see the Jorvik—'

Kate broke in impatiently, 'Rachel, I've just received a letter from Alice—she's told me some dreadful news about Angus, but there's so much she's left unsaid. Do you know anything about all this?'

There was a long pause the other end. Then, 'Oh, Kate, I was hoping you'd get your holiday over before hearing the news. But don't be too upset—it isn't as bad as it seems—'

'You don't know just how bad it is!' Kate answered, her voice rising with hysteria. 'I've been such a blind, tactless idiot, and Angus has every right to despise me, I said such awful things to him—things I didn't mean. What shall I do?'

'Kate, control yourself, try to calm down. Oh, I do wish I had time to talk to you—but my menfolk are waiting in the car for me, and Benjy is so excited already—if he gets too worked up he'll bring on one of his wheezy attacks.'

'Rachel, I'm coming back to Yelverthorpe straight away—I must see Angus as soon as possible. Do you know if he'll be in?'

'I expect so—he's home most days now. I don't know what's gone wrong between you two, but the only advice I can give is, beware of pity—that would be fateful. Bye now, Kate, and best of luck.'

I'll need more than luck, Kate told herself as she ran upstairs to pack her bag, I'll need the wisdom of Solomon and the enticing ways of Eve, and heaven help me, I'm short on both.

Less than two hours later she drew up outside the Queen Anne house in Damgate. The outer door stood open, and the inner door was on the latch. Kate rang, and when there was no answer, let herself in.

There was no mistaking that the mistress of the house was away. A jacket belonging to Angus was draped over the back of one chair, a pair of gardening boots was in the hearth, and papers were strewn all over the room. Alice would never have allowed that. The casement door leading on to the garden was wide open and Kate could hear the sounds of an axe in use. She walked through to the patio and saw Angus at the bottom of the garden hacking away at the lower branches of an old tree.

He wielded the axe as if it were a scourge, lashing away at the wood as if to inflict retribution of some kind. Kate saw his action as a symbol of his frustration—hacking away the dead wood as something useless, like his hands. Tears welled into her eyes at the notion. Those hands—those powerful clever hands with their healing touch—was that what he wanted to do to them? Destroy them because they could no longer serve him?

Then suddenly one blow went wide and the axe

fell from his grasp. He let out a mighty bellow of frustration and began to punch the tree with closed fists, swearing aloud as he did so.

It was almost unendurable to witness such impotent rage. Kate thought there was no more pitiful sight than a virile man at breaking-point. She thought of Rachel's words—beware of pity. But what was wrong with pity?

Shandy, who had been lolling near a smouldering bonfire, saw her approaching and came walking ponderously to greet her. Angus didn't look round, but he sensed her presence. Kate saw him tense, his broad shoulders grew rigid, then just as swiftly he relaxed, bracing himself to face her. He was grinning, but the hopeless look in his eyes clutched at her heart.

'I suppose you witnessed that unedifying display of temper? You see, I can't even hold a bloody axe any more.' His voice was sardonic, even defiant. 'But then you know that, don't you—you must have got Alice's letter by now. She told me she'd written to you when I called in to see her last night. Why have you come—to gloat? No! I had no right to say that, I apologise,' he looked at her under his heavy brows. 'We do enjoy tearing each other apart, don't we, Kate? We arouse deep passions in the other that are not always pleasant. But we won't dwell on the past, that's over and done with. Shall we cry quits?' He was trying so hard to be jocular, but it didn't quite come off.

All kinds of words were forming in Kate's mind—words of love and conciliation. She wanted to pour out her admiration for him, but nothing of this could she bring herself to utter aloud, instead she found herself telling him quite seriously that his hands were bleeding and something should be done about them.

Angus stared down at his knuckles with a mixture of surprise and curiosity. 'And I didn't even feel any pain! It must be true, that saying: where there's no sense there's no feeling.'

Kate's heart ached for him. This ghastly charade, how much longer could she carry it off? She took a minute handkerchief out of her pocket, and taking each of his hands in turn started to dab at the wounds.

'Are you trying to bathe my hands with your tears?' he asked sardonically.

'I can take all you can throw at me,' she retorted, her voice breaking on a sob. 'I came here to apologise—to beg you to forgive me for the wicked things I said—'

He interrupted her. 'Did this feeling of atonement come over you before or after you read Alice's letter?' he asked.

She looked at him with misty eyes. 'I know I deserve that, but I'm so terribly sorry—please believe that. Can't we pick up where we left off on Wednesday, before—before things started to go wrong?'

He looked tired, but not the tiredness of a man eaten up with inner grief—he was suffering from over-exertion. His shirt was patterned with patches of damp where he had perspired, and the red-gold hairs on his bared chest glistened with sweat. Kate heard him give a deep and unsettled sigh. 'I never could resist a woman's tears.' He looked at her, then gave a contrite smile. 'Come along then, let's have that talk now.'

There was no need to go indoors, there was a stone seat by the shrubbery, and they headed for that. Shandy padded after them and settled at their feet. Angus bent down, absentmindedly fondling the dog's ears. When he started to speak his voice was matter-of-fact, devoid of emotion.

He told her that before he had gone on holiday he had suspected there was something wrong with him, that he would sometimes have stiffness in his fingers and the joints would swell and cause pain. Then would come remissions, and he tried to convince himself there was nothing to worry about after all. But he couldn't put it out of his mind completely, so while he was in Scotland he took the opportunity to visit a rheumatologist, and was diagnosed as being in the early stages of rheumatoid arthritis. He knew what that meant—that eventually he would have to give up surgery.

'I took it hard at first,' he confessed. 'Then I thought—damn it, I'm not going to give in to it— I'll fight it and I'll work as long as I'm able. I was put to the test immediately we returned to Yelverthorpe when Alice fell and cracked her face.' He sat for a moment or two staring motionlessly at the ground. 'I nearly botched up that operation,' he said despairingly. 'Nobody knows how near I came to failure—what that would have meant to Alice. I could have been responsible for—Oh, hell, why think about it? I pulled it off, but only just, and that's what made me determined never to put another patient at risk again.'

'But the operation *was* a success—everybody said so—you were marvellous—' Kate stopped, seeing that her effort to reassure him was having no effect. He gave her an ironic smile.

'I was lucky, that's all—but enough of that. Well, I could still lecture, I could still teach, but that wasn't enough—I needed a challenge to keep me going, and then I thought of all the other sufferers with rheumatoid arthritis and allied complaints. I thought of remedial medicine; there's a lot can be done in that line for arthritic patients. I'm still a medical practitioner, a bit rusty perhaps, but I can remedy that. And I have one advantage in my favour which all those smart lads at the hospital haven't got. I shall know by personal experience what it's like on the other side of the coin. That should be of great benefit in my treatment of others. And that's how the idea of the McGill Remedial Clinic was born. There's still a lot of planning to be done, but I've got the premises—that's the main thing. And it's not going to be anything like a private nursing home, Kate.' He said this without rancour. 'There will be no fee-paying patients, though voluntary contributions will always be welcome. I've already been offered financial backing from three local business men, two of them ex-patients who felt they owed me something, God knows why! Still, it's something for me to get my teeth into, and that wasn't meant as a pun. It just slipped out,' and he laughed ruefully.

Instead of answering Kate did what she had been aching to do all along. She took his hands in hers and kissed each finger in turn.

'Is this a new kind of cure?' His voice was mocking, but his eyes pleaded with her.

'No, it's just my way of saying that I love you and have loved you for a long time, and it's because I love you so much that I made a fool of myself on Wednesday. I jumped to the wrong conclusions about your motive for giving up surgery. I'm bitterly sorry for misjudging you. I should have known you're not a bit like Martin.'

'You're not telling me this out of pity?' His words weren't quite as steady as he would have liked.

'Forget about pity!' she cried. 'What's the point of love without pity—without compassion? I'm asking you to have pity on *me*—I love you, and I don't even know if you love me in return.'

'Don't you, Kate? I thought I'd given myself away so many times. I couldn't believe that a pretty little thing like you would be attracted to a clumsy old grouch like me. Is the war over between us? No more harsh words—no more misunderstanding? Do you really want to marry me?' Angus's voice was teasing, but underlying it Kate could sense the deep self-doubt.

She put her head against his chest and kissed the place where she could feel his heart throbbing. 'I want to be more than a wife, my love,' she said huskily. 'I want to be a helpmate too—I want a job at the McGill Remedial Clinic. Could you bear to have me working with you?'

'Could I bear *not* to have you?' he echoed, his voice hoarse. 'Come here, my darling girl.' There was nothing lacking in the strength of his hands gripping her shoulders. Then, 'Kiss me, Kate!' he said, and gave her one of his old wolfish grins.

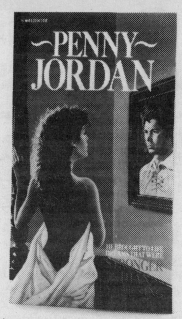

TAKE 4
DOCTOR NURSE ROMANCES

AND THRILL TO THE HEARTACHE AND DRAMA OF HOSPITAL LIFE.

THEY ARE YOURS **FREE!**

Reaching the end of a wonderful romantic story is always a little sad – even if it has a happy ending. So why not continue your reading pleasure with four marvellous Doctor Nurse stories – they're yours for the asking, absolutely free. It's our special offer to introduce you to Mills & Boon Reader Service. Thousands of regular romance readers use our subscription service. When you see the benefits you can enjoy as a subscriber we think you'd want to join them. See overleaf for details of our exciting FREE offer...

▶▶▶